St. Georges Church
Sunday School
1962/63

PRESENTED

TO

DONALD McAULAY

FOR

REGULAR ATTENDANCE

[signature]
(Supt)

Drummond Tract Depot, Stirling, Scotland.

THE SCARLET RAIDER

THE SCARLET RAIDER

by

JOSEPH B. ICENHOWER

COLLINS
LONDON AND GLASGOW

First printed in this edition 1963

PRINTED AND MADE IN GREAT BRITAIN BY
WM. COLLINS SONS AND CO. LTD.
LONDON AND GLASGOW

CONTENTS

CHAPTER ONE

ALL YANKEES MUST DIE

TIM MORGAN pulled the collar of his old army jacket up close around his neck and clucked sympathetically to the ancient horse pulling the light wagon. A steady rain had brought a sharp drop in the temperature, unseasonably low for April in northern Virginia. The narrow road, hemmed in on both sides by a thick forest of glistening pines, was a rut-filled morass of sticky mud.

"Ain't much farther, Nellie," he called down encouragingly from his high seat on the wagon. He darted a quick glance over his shoulder to the lonesome road behind him. Somehow he could not get rid of the uneasy feeling that kept gnawing at his chest. Reckon I'm just more scary than usual to-day, he thought. Of course he always was a little jumpy returning home, even though he had made the trip through the Yankee lines into Fairfax County Courthouse dozens of times. There wasn't a turn or a pothole on Little River Turnpike that he did not know like the back of his hand. He could not help grinning to himself when he thought of how he had fooled the blue-coat soldiers all winter long. What if they guessed he'd been carrying contraband all this time!

Nellie snorted in protest as she leaned forward in the harness to draw the wagon up a slight grade. Tim's grin vanished when he remembered the picket line just over the rise. Involuntarily he put his hand down on the seat to smooth out the black oilskin cover. The pickets, vedettes they were usually called, had never done more than ask him a few questions, but he always expected them to order him down from the seat. If they made a really thorough inspection, they would be sure to find the false bottom in the seat. The mere thought of what would happen made his spine crawl.

Pa kept telling him that Abe Lincoln was too soft to let his bluecoats hang a kid, especially a sixteen-year-old. Sometimes Tim wished he could believe this as easily as his pa. Anyway he had to carry on. He and Pa had worked too long on the plan to let anything short of discovery stop them now. Pa had moved to Cub Run to be nearer the Federal lines, and between them they had set up a couple of trips to Fairfax every week for more than two months.

The Yankees were accustomed to seeing Tim on the road and in town. Only when the trips began to look routine did he start to carry contraband. Every venture now meant helping the South lick the Yankees. He shifted uneasily on the seat and remembered what was in the flat parcels under him this time. "Drugs," Mr. Moore, the secret Confederate agent, had whispered when he slid them into the wagon back at Fairfax. Morphine, Tim reckoned. With the Federal navy blockading the coast, the doctors with the Army of Northern Virginia were practically begging for supplies. He was glad to be carrying drugs; this gave him the feeling of really helping. He remembered the long line of wagons carrying the wounded south after the last battle and how helpless he had felt because he was too young to join the army. When the chance came to act as an agent, he did not hesitate, although secretly he would rather stand up with the soldiers and fight like a man. Pa said every time he brought a load of contraband back through the lines he struck a blow for the Confederacy, but he reckoned the Yankees would think he was no more than a spy.

Nellie heard the horse behind them before he did. Tim watched her ears straighten up, and instinctively he shot a quick glance over his shoulder. His heart began to race at the sight of a blue-clad cavalryman pounding up the road after him. For a moment he wondered whether Mr. Moore had been discovered. He hunched down on his seat and kept his eyes on Nellie's ears.

"Whoa! Whoa, I say! You mangy dog!"

The trooper brought his foam-flecked mount to a skidding halt with a savage sawing motion of the reins.

Tim halted Nellie with a soft command, then turned to face the trooper with the most innocent look he could muster. He recognised the man instantly as one of the corporals stationed at the picket post up ahead. This thought brought an instant sense of relief. The Yankee was probably on his way back to his post. It was not likely that he was chasing the wagon.

"You're that Rebel kid, Morgan, ain't ye?"

Tim nodded. He had heard the other pickets call this man Bull, and he didn't like his looks. The trooper's bleary eyes darted over the wagon as he slouched in his saddle.

"Saw ye come to town." The cavalryman leered, nodding his head drunkenly. "Make the trip two, sometimes three times a week, don't ye?"

Tim stirred uneasily on the seat and nodded again, almost afraid to speak.

"Ain't ye got a tongue?"

"Yes—yes, sir," replied the boy.

The trooper edged his horse in alongside the wagon. Reaching down, he grabbed the corner of the worn canvas covering the few supplies and threw it back with a sweep of his hand. He let his eyes flick over the sack of corn meal, the sack of oats Tim had bought for Nellie, and the worn horse-shoes scattered on the wagon bed.

"Don't eat too good down your way, eh, kid?"

"No, sir," Tim replied, taut with anxiety. This half-drunken Yankee was getting too nosey. He watched the bull-like figure warily as he brought his horse up alongside the seat. The trooper leaned over and fixed sly eyes on Tim.

"Could be ye'd eat a lot better if you'n me could do a little business."

"I—I don't know what you mean," Tim stammered.

Bull stared at the boy thoughtfully. "Folks over your way need lotsa things—food, guns—fer huntin', that is, and," he groped for more necessities of life, "and medicine."

Tim felt fear, cold fear, for the first time. He tried to keep his eyes steady on the man's face. "Yes, sir," he replied. "They sure need food all right." He kept his voice as level as he could. "Could Pa'n me get hold of a few dollars now and then we could eat whole heaps better."

The trooper snorted in disgust. "I'm talkin' big money, kid." Reaching into his coat pocket, he pulled out a half-filled bottle, tilted his head back, drained the contents, then hurled the empty bottle into the pines. He wiped his mouth with the back of his hand and leaned over Tim again.

"Big money, kid," he repeated. "I got a feller lined up who'll git all the stuff I can pass along. You bin in and out o' the lines ever' few days. I give you the stuff and you peddle it t'other side."

"I can't do that, sir," Tim protested. "That's contraband, sir. The pickets'd shoot me sure if they caught me with that kind of stuff!"

Bull grinned. "I got that figgered out too. I'll fix it so's I get the picket duty when you're comin' through."

Tim thought desperately as the trooper waited for a reply. Here he was already running supplies through the lines, and now the enemy offered him a chance to run through twice as much. If he said no, Bull might do anything in a drunken rage. On the other hand he couldn't very well say yes to the plan until after he'd talked with Pa. Worse still, he thought, Bull might make things tougher for him at the picket post if he turned down the scheme completely. He'd better take a middle course.

"I don't rightly know, sir. I reckon I could sell some food to the folks over Cub Run way. I——"

"Food!" Bull snorted. "Them Rebels'll pay big fer things they can't git. Little things you kin find a hidin' place fer in the wagon. Things like a pistol maybe——"

Tim hedged again. "I'll have to talk to Pa," he replied.

The burly trooper fixed him with a cold stare. "You do that, kid. You do just that," he said softly. He reached over and grabbed Tim's arm in a vice-like grip. "How much did ye git fer that stuff ye took to town?"

"Four dollars, sir." Tim winced as the man's fingers dug deep into his arm.

"Lemme see it," the trooper demanded.

Tim reached into his pocket with his free hand and drew out a few coins. "That's all I got left," he said.

"Gimme!" Bull grabbed the coins, sneered at the measly change and jammed it into his pocket. "Ye kin tell yer pa what'll happen to ye ever' time ye come to town if he says we can't do business t'gether." He shifted his eyes to the patient Nellie. "Now git that bag o' bones movin'. I'll see ye to th' picket line." He laid his hand on the butt of his holstered pistol. "I'd advise ye to keep yer mouth shut when we git there," he warned.

The next quarter of a mile seemed the longest drive that Tim had ever made. Bull dropped behind the wagon and followed it slowly along the road. Although he did not dare turn around, Tim felt the trooper's gaze boring right through him. He'd sure be glad to get through the picket line and on home so he could tell Pa about the Yankee's proposition. Pa would know what to do, he hoped.

Just over the rise he could see a small camp-fire in the clearing occupied by the pickets. As the wagon drew closer, he saw a trooper move out to the road and stand by the pivoted log that the Yankees had swung across the turnpike as a gate. The man was Murphy, sergeant of the group.

Murphy grinned. "Well now, 'tis the lad on his way home," he called out.

Scared as he was, Tim forced a smile. Murphy's grin was infectious. The boy figured he could almost like the big Irishman. Too bad he was a Yankee.

Murphy's eyes narrowed when he recognised Bull coming up from behind the wagon. " 'Tis poor company ye keep, lad," he said, his eyes taking in the corporal's condition.

"I heard that, ye thickheaded Irishman," Bull growled.

" 'Twas meant fer yer ears as well as the lad's, ye sotted disgrace to the uniform ye wear."

Angrily Bull threw himself from his mount and faced the sergeant.

Tim watched the half-dozen soldiers around the camp-fire scramble to their feet, viewing the scene at the wagon.

"Sure and 'tis time ye returned t' duty," Murphy said in a level voice. "Noon-time ye were posted fer duty, not four hours later, and I might say it'll give me great pleasure to report yer absence to the lieutenant."

"Why you——!" Bull raised a massive fist.

"If it's trouble yer seekin' . . ." Murphy warned.

Bull lurched forward, his fist swinging in a wide arc. Murphy shifted to one side, parried the blow with his left and sent his right smashing into Bull's jaw. The blow almost lifted the man off his feet. Eyes glazing over, he fell face down in the mud.

Murphy glanced contemptuously at the motionless figure, then flashed a quick grin at Tim.

"Ye must have discipline in an army, lad." Nodding towards the sprawled corporal he added, "Mostly fer the likes o' him." He reached into the wagon and threw back the canvas covering. He glanced at the few supplies, then covered them up again.

"All right, lad, be off with ye. Keep yer horse movin' and ye kin make it home 'fore dark." He glanced at the boy's taut face. "Wait a minute," he ordered and walked over to the fire. He returned with a loaf of white bread and tossed it up to the boy.

"I can't——" Tim started to protest.

"Sure ye can, lad. The Grand Army of the Potomac won't be missin' a bite o' bread."

"Thank you, Mr. Murphy," muttered Tim. He was close to tears as Nellie leaned forward to get the wagon moving.

Half an hour later, just after the wagon clattered over the wooden bridge crossing Cub Run, Tim pulled off the turnpike into a faint trace leading through the pines. Although the road was dark within the forest, Nellie had no difficulty picking her way along the familiar trail. To his relief Tim smelled smoke, because even though he had munched half the loaf of bread, he was still hungry. A dog's muffled bark sounded up ahead. Prince apparently heard them coming. Nellie quickened her pace. The forest no longer seemed oppressive. Tim could almost smell supper on the fire.

Abruptly the trail entered a stump-studded clearing.

Tim glanced with satisfaction at freshly turned earth between the blackened stumps. He and Pa'd got the spring ploughing done in good time. Up ahead, square in the centre of the open space, a long low cabin, its logs black in the semi-darkness, sat low on the ground. On one side a stone chimney hugged the logs, its top rising a few feet above the peaked roof. Along the rear wall a lean-to slanted against the logs. There the ground sloped gently towards a small stream swollen by the afternoon rain. Roiling waters echoed through the clearing with a steady swishing sound. Near the rough-hewn boards of the front door, a nondescript hound tugged at a frayed rope, dancing happily as the wagon creaked to a halt. Tim jumped down and ruffled the dog's ears, then he saw his father standing in the doorway.

"Any trouble, son?" Ben Morgan asked, his gaze steady on the shivering boy.

One look at his father's calm face and most of Tim's fears disappeared. He remembered how Jeb Stuart had once said that Ben Morgan was the finest cavalryman in the South, especially when under fire. That his father was no longer the dashing cavalryman of a year before was apparent as he moved forward awkwardly, a hickory peg instead of a right leg sinking into the mud with every step. He moved up to the horse's head and stroked her muzzle with a true cavalryman's affection for a faithful mount.

"Go on in the house and warm yourself, Tim. I'll put Nellie up and feed her."

"Thanks, Pa."

Tim heaved the sacks over his shoulder and turned

towards the cabin. He hesitated briefly, undecided whether to take up the matter of Bull's scheme with his father then. Better wait, he thought to himself as he saw his father ease Nellie out of the traces.

"The sutler's stuff is under the front seat, Pa," he called.

"I'll fetch it in," Pa answered over his shoulder.

Tim pushed aside the heavy door and entered the dimly lit cabin. He dropped the sacks near the glowing fireplace and hung his coat on a peg thrust into the clay between the logs. Over the fire a pot hung from an iron arm on a pivot. He picked up a forked stick and pulled the pot out over the hearth. The rich brown gravy simmering around dark chunks of venison gave off a satisfying aroma. Tim reached for a battered pewter plate, ladled out a generous helping of the stew, and carried it to the pine table in the centre of the bare but clean room. He broke off a chunk of the loaf of bread Mr. Murphy had given him, and dipped it in the brown gravy. It tasted good even though it was Yankee bread!

Tim's father came in the cabin before his son had finished his meal. An outsider would have remarked at once the similarity of the two. Both had the same clear blue eyes and light, almost blond eyebrows. The straight Morgan nose above a wide, firm mouth was characteristic of both. True, the boy's face—and for that matter his whole body—needed filling out, but the promise of a rather sturdy though not tall build was there.

Tim watched his father lay three flat parcels wrapped in oilcloth on the table and slowly begin to remove the covering. The first parcel was a black box. When his father opened it, he gave a pleased exclamation at the sight of the fine Sheffield-steel surgical instruments fitted neatly within.

"The army command will be mighty happy with this, Tim," he remarked. "Any doctor would be proud to own this set."

"Let's look at the other packages, Pa."

Ben Morgan quickly broke the seals. Tim leaned over and saw several rows of neatly packed glass vials.

"It's drugs, the man told me," he said.

His father held one of the glass cylinders up to the faint light of the single candle on the table. "Yes, morphine," he answered. "Lord knows the troops can use this." He raised his eyes and stared thoughtfully across the room.

Tim knew his father was thinking about the time the surgeon had taken off his leg. Trooper friends had told Tim all about the ordeal—how his father, stretched out on the operating table, had put a rifle-ball between his teeth to chew on and told the doctor to go ahead. Although the field surgeon had nothing to relieve the pain, his father had not made a sound during the operation. Tim prized the lead ball that Ben Morgan's friends had picked up afterwards. It was as flat as a penny.

"We'd best get these things wrapped up again and hidden away, Tim," his father cut in. "I'd hate to lose them now. That morphine's going to help some poor devil when the pain gets real bad. A man doesn't suffer too much even with a bad wound if the doctor has some of this to give him." He folded the oilcloth around the boxes and handed them to the boy. "Put 'em in the cache, son."

Tim carried the contraband to the hearth and prised up a flat stone. He removed it carefully to prevent chipping, then scooped up the dirt underneath until he found the handle of a metal box. Pushing the dirt away carefully, he lifted the box out of its hole and placed the parcels inside. Just as carefully he replaced the box and covered it with earth, then put the stone in place. He brushed away the small particles of loose dirt remaining on the hearth and stood back to survey his handiwork. A nosey Yank would find it difficult to discover anything amiss about the hearth.

"We won't have long to wait this time, son. Mosby said he'd send some of the boys over to-night to take the stuff off our hands."

"Do you think Captain Mosby will come himself, Pa?" Tim asked, eager at the mention of Virginia's famous Ranger captain.

His father smiled. "I don't know, Tim. John Mosby can't be everywhere at once, though I suspect the Yankees think he is."

Tim's father knew that every youngster in Virginia, including Tim, worshipped the fabulous captain. Operating for the most part within enemy country, Mosby's successful raids on Yankee trains, supply lines, and even heavily guarded bivouac areas had captured the imagination of the entire South. Federal commanders considered the raider no better than an outlaw and, without exception, promised to hang him on the spot if captured.

"Pa."

"What is it, son?" But he knew what was coming.

"You don't think the Yankees would really hang Captain Mosby, do you?"

Ben Morgan smiled. "They have to catch him first."

"No, I mean it, Pa. Do you really believe they would hang him like an outlaw if they caught him?"

His father frowned. "They'd have no right, Tim. Mosby's a captain in the Confederate Army. He always wears a uniform too—even when he's slippin' through the Yank lines."

"But I heard the soldiers in Fairfax say they'd hang him if they got their hands on him," Tim insisted.

A glint came into his father's eyes.

"If they hang either Mosby or any of his men, they'll wish they hadn't." Ben Morgan glanced at his son and broke into a grin. "You let Mosby worry about that, Tim. He can take care of himself. Now tell me about your trip."

Tim frowned. Slowly he recited the events of the day. He saw his father's face grow tense when he told of his encounter with the cavalryman, Bull, but then relax into a smile when he heard how Murphy had dropped the corporal in the mud.

"Your friend Murphy sounds like a good man."

"But, Pa, he's a Yankee!"

Ben Morgan chuckled. "Yankees are like everyone else, son. Some good, some bad." He noticed the boy's puzzled look. "Good or bad though, Tim, we can't make distinctions; we're fighting the whole kit and kaboodle."

Tim felt relieved. He did not like to hear Pa talk like that. Look what the Yankees had done to him! Made him a cripple. Bitterly the boy remembered that dark night a year ago . . . himself and his mother struggling through the windswept forest on the side of Oak Mountain, driving the livestock into hiding . . . and down below, their burning farmhouse lighting up the countryside, as a cold driving wind spread the flames to the outbuildings. His mother's cough had started that night and had persisted until her death a month later. Dead, actually, because she had sheltered Rangers hard-pressed by blue-clad cavalry. Yes, Yankees were meant to be killed!

His father's voice interrupted Tim's memories. "This scheme Bull suggests . . . We better hadn't turn him down completely. We'll try to stall him off without making him mad. I'll admit it's risky but we may have to play along with him some." He thought for a minute. "We'll get word to Mosby. Maybe he can think of something."

Suddenly Prince, stretched out near the fire, raised his head and gave a low growl.

"Quiet, Prince," Tim's father ordered. He reached over and snuffed out the candle with his thumb and forefinger. "Someone's comin'. Don't let Nellie make any noise," he cautioned and moved quickly to the door. Easing it open, he slipped out into the night.

CHAPTER TWO

PARTISAN CHIEF

TIM CROSSED to the low door in the back wall of the cabin and ducked into the lean-to. Murmuring softly to the horse, he held her nostrils to prevent her from neighing. He stood motionless for a few minutes, then finally heard the muted call of a hoot owl in the forest. Seconds later, an answering hoot came from near the cabin. He heard the front door open and his father's voice:

"Help me get some candles lit, son. We got company."

Tim hurried back into the cabin and helped his father. Within the minute he heard horses stamping in the clearing. His father moved to the door and threw it wide open.

"Come in, gentlemen. It's a pleasure."

Tim's mouth dropped open when he saw the first man sweep into the room. It was Mosby himself!

John Singleton Mosby weighed barely 125 pounds, but he gave the impression of being a bigger man. A sweeping ostrich plume curled back from his grey slouch hat. As the raider threw back his scarlet-lined cape, Tim saw two heavily studded Colt pistols in twin holsters. Although the man carried no sabre, he wore a yellow cavalry sash wrapped tightly about his waist. When he swept off his hat, he looked older than his twenty-eight years. Then for the first time the raider's eyes looked into Tim's. They were blue, hard as ice and just as cold. Suddenly he smiled and put out his hand.

"You're Tim."

"Y-yes, sir," Tim stammered as he took the outstretched hand.

"You're doing a fine job."

Tim flushed with pleasure at the praise.

Mosby turned to Ben Morgan and placed an arm around his shoulder. "Chip off the old block, eh, Ben?" he said affectionately.

"He's doing all right," Tim's father said, then faced the half-dozen other Rangers who had entered the cabin. "Been coffee on the fire if I'd known when you were comin', boys." He moved towards the fireplace. "It won't take long, I'll . . ."

"There's no time, Ben. We've got a long ride ahead." Mosby smiled a thin smile. "Yankees north of here are letting us have some horses."

Ben Morgan grinned. "They don't know it, I'll bet."

"Not yet," Mosby answered.

The other troopers broke into smiles.

"Get the packages, Tim," his father ordered.

Tim hurried to the hearth and dug out the black boxes. He carried them to the centre of the room and placed them on the table.

"Look at this." Tim's father unwrapped the parcels.

The Ranger captain's eyes lighted up when he saw the gleaming surgical instruments. He picked one up and turned it over slowly in his hands.

"With instruments like these I think I could dig out a

Minié ball myself." He fixed Tim with a direct look. "It's not just that we can get medical supplies through the lines, Tim. What's more important is that with established contacts on the other side we can get information and perhaps other much needed contraband. I don't mean to say these medical supplies aren't important." He laid a hand on the boy's shoulder. "On the contrary, this is a fine haul, and you are fast becoming one of our best agents."

"John," Ben Morgan spoke up. "Until to-day Tim has had no trouble, but I'm afraid he's run into complications."

He quickly outlined the boy's encounter with the Federal trooper, Bull.

Mosby listened carefully, then turned again to the boy.

"You acted wisely, son. I'm afraid we'll have to go along with this Bull—at least far enough to keep him quiet. We can't use a man of his calibre for long though." His face darkened momentarily. "If he gets too troublesome, we'll have to take care of him. In the meantime, don't take any chances!"

"I won't, sir," replied Tim, then mustering his courage, blurted out, "Sir, when can I join your command?" Seeing the frown on the captain's forehead, he went on hurriedly, "I can ride and I'm a good shot, sir."

The Ranger captain surveyed him from head to foot.

"I'm sure you can," he replied thoughtfully. "But right now you're worth as much as any trooper in my command." He hesitated a second, then asked, "How old are you, Tim?"

"Fifteen, sir," Tim answered, then added quickly, "I'll be sixteen in June."

"Hmm," mused the captain. "There are soldiers in the line as young." He glanced briefly at Tim's father.

Ben Morgan shrugged.

"Do you have pen and paper, Ben?" Mosby asked.

Tim's father clumped over to a wooden box in a corner of the cabin and returned with a quill pen, ink, and paper. He placed them on the table. Mosby sat down, wrote hurriedly, then stood up and handed the paper to the boy.

"If your father approves, here's evidence of your attachment to my command. I haven't dated it because right now I need you in your present capacity. The Federals would hang you as a spy if they caught you inside their lines while actually a member of my command." He watched Tim's face fall. "It won't be much longer, son. Your job here will soon be finished."

Tim and his father exchanged quick glances.

Captain Mosby watched their unbelieving faces with amusement. "Don't you think the Yankees have been on Virginia soil long enough?"

Tim saw his father look long at the Ranger as if trying to figure out what was in his mind.

"You aim to push the Federals back across the Potomac, John?"

"Might not have to push them back; might just lead them back," the captain answered quietly.

Ben Morgan scratched his head. "I don't see . . ."

"Come, Ben, if your force is insufficient for a frontal attack, what is the next best course of action?" Mosby asked.

"A surprise attack behind, I reckon," he replied.

"Of course. That's what I've been doing for months —on a small scale perhaps, but with some success."

"No one would disagree with you there, John," Tim's father said. "But movin' a few men at night is not the same as movin' an army."

"Suppose you kept your army behind the Blue Ridge Mountains and moved it north up the Shenandoah Valley?"

Ben Morgan nodded.

"Then suppose you kept your cavalry between the Blue Ridge and Cub Mountains. There's only three passes through Cub Mountains . . . hold 'em with cavalry and the army'd be in Maryland before the Yankees knew they were moving."

Ben Morgan chuckled. "And when they finally found out that the army was moving north, the politicians in Washington would yell for the whole Union Army to protect them."

"Right," Mosby answered.

Tim's father frowned. "But do you think Lee would risk an invasion?"

"General Lee doesn't have much choice. He has to take a gambler's chance," Mosby answered. "We need horses and supplies badly."

Tim thought of the rich farm land of central Pennsylvania, and the great store of supplies and transport held in the supply centres of the northern state. If the Confederates could get their hands on those stores, General Lee would have a well-equipped army. The plan sure sounded dangerous though. He looked at the calm, poised Ranger. If Lee had many men like him, the army could get away with such a scheme.

Mosby drew on his white gauntlets and moved towards the door.

"I've brought you some 'Southern heirlooms' the Yankees love to buy. Tim can take them through the lines a few at a time. Save you sending food in. Tim can pass the word around that the families down this way are disposing of their valuables in order to get food." He smiled. "What the bluecoats don't know is that we got the stuff from them in the first place."

Ben Morgan roared with laughter. "No doubt some Yankee general's silver."

"This particular general thought it appropriate to have his entire staff dine on his own plate," Mosby answered. "Unfortunately for him, his mess officer fell behind the line of march. We merely appropriated the wagon."

Tim's admiring glance swept the smiling faces of the Rangers in the room. The captain made the feat sound very simple, yet Tim could visualise the wild dash of these same men into the supply train, as they cut out the wagons and made off with them before the protecting Yankees could rally their forces. His heart skipped a beat when he rememberd that perhaps very soon he might be one of them.

The troopers moved out of the cabin. Tim and his father followed them into the clearing. One of the Rangers pulled two gunny sacks from behind his saddle and handed them to Ben Morgan. Mosby walked over to his horse and took a holster and cavalryman's Colt pistol out of his saddle-bags. He turned and handed them to Tim.

"Here's your first equipment, Ranger . . . Compliments of another Yankee general!"

With a wave of his gauntleted hand he swung up into his saddle and led his men at a gallop out of the clearing.

The sheet of paper clutched in his hand, Tim ran into the cabin and read the bold writing by candle-light.

To Whom It May Concern:

Reposing special trust and confidence in the patriotism and ability of Timothy Morgan, I, John Singleton Mosby, Captain of the Provisional Army of the Confederate States of America, do hereby appoint him a trooper in my command.

Given under my hand in the field.

signed
J. S. MOSBY

"You couldn't ride with a better man, son," his father said quietly.

Tim nodded as he folded the paper. He went to the fireplace and placed both the gun and the document in the secret compartment. While the boy busied himself at the fireplace, his father dumped the contents of Mosby's sacks on the table. Tim heard him give a sharp exclamation as the various heirlooms gleamed in the candle-light. For the most part they were silver: candlesticks, serving pieces, cruets, although there were several gold-leaf picture frames. Using only a few at a time, the two Morgans would have trade goods to take through the lines for some time to come. No longer would they have to part with their own meagre supplies to provide a reason for the trips.

Tim felt a momentary touch of fear as he surveyed the treasures. Even if the Yankees did swallow his story about his friends selling off their silver, he would have Bull to reckon with. Once the greedy trooper caught sight of that gleaming silver, he'd be hard to put off. Tim looked up and caught his father's eyes.

"This trooper called Bull, son, if he stops you, give him any money you get for the stuff."

"But, Pa!"

"No buts about it, Tim. The money's not important; what you're doing for the South is."

Tim picked up a silver tray and turned it over in the light of the candle. Its shiny surface reflected the yellow light. Such a valuable piece should bring a lot of money—money, he and Pa could use. He set his face stubbornly. He'd think of some way to keep from turning it over to a Yankee, especially one as mean as Bull.

CHAPTER THREE

CAUGHT!

IT WAS hard to realise that only two days ago the turnpike had been one mudhole after the other, thought Tim as Nellie pulled the wagon along with more pep than she had shown in months. A fellow could hardly believe there was a war goin' on, what with the birds singin' and all. He'd even seen two rabbits. They'd just sat and watched him until he was almost on them. Didn't act scared at all.

One of the wheels hit a rock and Tim heard the clink of silver in the gunny sack behind. His mood darkened. Suppose the Yankees didn't believe his story? He shook the thought off. After all, folks down his way were hungry—if they had any silver left they might sell it for food. He stared up ahead as the wagon rounded a turn. The picket station was not more than a couple of hundred yards ahead.

Suddenly he recognised the trooper at the gate. It was Bull Ruffing! Just his luck! Tim thought of turning back, but the man stood in the middle of the road facing his way. To turn now would surely invite suspicion. He gripped the reins and kept moving.

"Figgered ye'd be showin' up soon," Bull said, as Tim pulled Nellie to a halt. After placing his carbine against a log and walking to the wagon, Bull glanced contemptuously at the lone gunny sack.

"You Rebels must be scrapin' the bottom o' th' bar'l." He reached out a ham-like fist and dragged the sack towards him. His expression changed to bewilderment when he felt the sack. With a quick jerk he broke the tie string and stared into the bag. Bull gave a low whistle as his eyes ran over the contents: an old but sparkling candelabrum, a small silver dish, and an exquisite miniature picture frame.

The trooper darted a look over his shoulder at the cluster of small tents in the picket area. Tim followed his glance and saw Murphy approaching.

"Where'd ye git this stuff, kid?" Bull asked in a low, hoarse voice. He shot another look at the approaching sergeant, then muttered, "I'll see ye later."

"Top o' the mornin' to ye, Tim lad," the big Irishman called, a wide smile on his red face. "And what are ye takin' t' market this day?" He walked up to the wagon bed and glanced into the open sack. "Faith, lad, whose home did ye rob?" he exclaimed when he saw the silver.

"I didn't rob any home, sir. Missus Randolph, who lives over our way, needs hard money awful bad." That was true, Tim thought. The Randolphs had given all they owned to the Confederate Army.

Murphy picked up the silver dish and examined it closely.

" 'Tis a bad way the good woman's in to be partin' with the likes o' these," he said sympathetically. "However, they should bring the lady a pretty penny."

"I hope so, sir."

"Mind ye be careful, lad, that nobody steals 'em from ye." Murphy turned to Bull. "Let the lad through,

Bull Ruffing," His eyes narrowed as he saw Ruffing stare greedily at the bag. "And be quick about it!"

Bull favoured his sergeant with a hate-filled look and, swaggering insolently, swung the log off the road to let the boy pass. As the wagon drew abreast of him, he gave Tim a sly wink.

Tim drove on with a sense of foreboding; it would be his luck to find Bull on the gate to-day. Now he'd never be able to stall the surly corporal. From the way he stared at the silver Tim was sure Bull would meet him again on the way home. Maybe he could wait on the road in the hope that one of the other pickets would be coming out from town in the late afternoon. If none did, he'd just have to give Bull whatever he got for the silver. He leaned back and filled his lungs with the brisk morning air.

The weather was too fine to let him worry long, and by the time Tim sighted the first houses on the outskirts of Fairfax, he had forgotten his fears. Ahead lay the headquarters of the 18th Pennsylvania and some companies of the 1st Vermont, both cavalry units. The village streets were alive with mounted men. Tim guessed that the Yankees were not taking any more chances. Just three weeks before, Mosby and twenty-eight of his men had entered the town under cover of darkness and had captured Brigadier General Stoughton in his bed. In a move that had the whole South holding its sides with laughter, he took the general back through the lines and handed him over to Confederate General Fitzhugh Lee. With the present activity and reinforcements now in the village, Tim reckoned the Yanks could not easily be fooled again.

When the wagon reached the junction of Little River Turnpike and the Centerville Road, Tim spotted the vari-coloured sutler's wagons parked near the court-house. He drove on until he spied Mr. Moore, a short, rather plain man with a heavy black beard. He heaved a sigh of relief. At least the Yanks had not caught on to him yet! His black-clad figure looked mighty good as he waved and started walking towards the wagon.

Tim stopped well clear of any idlers and waited for Moore to join him.

Tom Moore was one of the Confederacy's most valuable agents. In his role as a sutler he was free to follow the army with his well-stocked wagon. Sutlers were a tolerated evil in both armies, inasmuch as they carried for the soldier's needs items that the commissary departments could not or would not furnish.

"Mornin', Tim." Tom Moore purposely spoke in a loud voice for the benefit of any loungers who might be listening. "Bring any of those fine hams in to-day? Get you a good price for 'em, son. There's no one like Tom Moore to get the best price, I allus say."

"Sorry, sir. We didn't have any hams, but I do have some of the neighbour's stuff I'd like you to sell for me." He pointed to the sack in the wagon bed. "Maybe you could tell me who might buy these."

"I'm your man," Moore replied heartily. "Yes, siree, son. I'm the man who can get you the best price in town." He reached out and opened the sack. Tim saw his eyes widen in astonishment.

"Folks are gettin' hungry down our way, Mr. Moore," Tim explained. "Can't eat stuff like that."

Tom Moore stroked his black beard. Out of the

corner of his eye he saw several soldiers approaching the wagon. His mouth widened in a big grin.

"Drive right over there by my wagon, sonny, and we'll make a trade," he said with his former heartiness. He picked up the gunny sack and threw it over his shoulder. "Yes, siree, sonny, honest Tom Moore'll give you a better price than any other man in Fairfax."

Tim heard the soldiers snicker as they passed by. He picked up the reins and urged Nellie into a slow walk towards the court-house. He pulled her in alongside Moore's vividly painted store-on-wheels and jumped to the ground.

"Whose hare-brained idea is this, Tim?" Moore asked in a low voice. "You're bound to attract attention if you bring stuff like this into Fairfax."

"Like I said, Mr. Moore, folks down our way are gettin' powerful hungry." Tim glanced around quickly to make sure no one was close. "It's Captain Mosby's idea, sir. Says it may fool the Yankees into thinking people are so hungry they're about to give up." He let that idea sink in for a moment. "Captain figures that being Yankees the officers might let me move around camps more, maybe even headquarters, if they smell a bargain."

"Sounds like Mosby." Moore nodded. "Guess it makes sense too." He fixed Tim with a steady look. "Puts you in more of a spot, though. Have to keep wide-awake." He paused, then went on. "Tell you what I'll do. There's a couple of Yankee officers here in town that'll pay good money for these. You scoot off and buy whatever you and your pa need." He reached in his pocket and pulled out several bills. "This'll take care of whatever you want. Give me at least a couple of hours to get rid of the silver."

Tim accepted the offer quickly. Although only a village, Fairfax had taken on the air of a city, due to the great influx of troops. The town's only hotel now served as a Federal hospital. The larger homes, including Doctor Gunnel's fine brick mansion, housed the officers. Tim deliberately appraised the soldiers on the street and noted that most of them wore the regimentals of the 18th Pennsylvania and 1st Vermont, but scattered here and there were a few troopers of the 5th New York. Captain Mosby would want that information.

After wandering around for an hour or so, Tim entered the general store and made his purchases. He spent all the money that Moore had given him. He fully expected Bull Ruffing would take what he had left anyway, and there wasn't any use saving it. He even bought a new store-made pipe for Pa, figuring he had good reason to be a spendthrift. Leaving the store, he wandered back to the court-house yard where Moore was waiting for him. Tim tossed his supplies into the wagon and faced the agent.

"Like I said, Tim, no trouble gettin' rid of your bargains. The officers jumped at the chance to buy them." Reluctantly he handed Tim a wad of green backs. "I still don't like it much, Tim. Maybe it'll give you a good excuse to come to town often, but there's many a man who'd kill you for less than that. There's thirty dollars there."

Tim took the money. He had not realised there would be so much. For a moment he thought maybe he'd better tell Mr. Moore about Bull Ruffing. On the other hand, there wasn't anything Moore could do about it. He had enough on his hands without getting involved in Tim's troubles. He'd hide part of the money and give Bull the rest if he stopped him. The bully would be suspicious if he didn't get any.

"I'll be all right, Mr. Moore," Tim reassured the man. "I've made the trip so many times now the Yankees are used to seeing me."

Moore shook his head slowly. "I still don't like it. If anyone jumps you, give 'em the money. Don't argue!"

"I won't, sir. Don't worry."

They shook hands and Tim climbed up on the wagon seat and pulled out of the courtyard. He let Nellie take her own pace; the road was dry and the pulling was easy for her.

About a mile from the picket post Tim began to think about what he would do if Bull met him. Not a single soldier had passed him on the road, and when he entered the heavily forested area, the boy began to look uneasily over his shoulder. He had not seen Bull in town but that did not mean the trooper hadn't been there. He looked back at the road again, expecting to see the cavalryman pounding after him any minute. He sensed something was wrong. For one thing, he didn't hear any birds singing. Everything seemed too quiet, until Bull's sinister voice sounded:

"You can stop right here, kid."

Tim jerked his head around in time to see Bull Ruffing step out of the pines on to the road. The trooper grabbed Nellie's bridle and jerked her to a halt.

"I—I didn't see you, sir," Tim stammered.

"Reckon ye didn't." The trooper leered. "Ole Bull's

bin waitin' fer ye." He moved up alongside the wagon seat. "How much did ye git fer that silver?"

"I've got ten dollars here, sir," replied Tim. He reached into his pocket and pulled out ten greenbacks. "I had to buy some things me'n Pa needed."

"Yer lyin', kid." Bull's face darkened in anger.

"There's only ten dollars, sir." Tim pulled his pockets inside out. "You can search me if you don't believe me."

"Shut up."

Bull glared at the boy, then glanced into the wagon bed.

"What'd ye spend the money fer, ya little——" He reached over and threw the canvas off Tim's supplies, then put one foot on the wheel and climbed up into the wagon. With a savage kick he scattered the gunny sacks.

"I ought to——"

His words were cut short by a booming voice.

"Ye ought to what, ye thievin' scum?"

Bull spun around. Murphy was standing between the trees at the edge of the road.

"Where'd ya come from, Irishman?" Bull blustered. He watched the sergeant warily as he moved towards the wagon.

"I followed ye through the woods from camp, knowin' yer thievin' nature," the Irishman said. " 'Tis low scum ye are, taking th' lad's few dollars. But of course yer thievin' days are over. I'm puttin' ye under arrest."

Tim watched Murphy move up slowly to the side of the wagon, his eyes never leaving the corporal.

"Now, Murphy, ye wouldn't turn in one of yer own men." Bull's scowling face relaxed into a fawning smile. "Why Murphy, we bin through a lot together. 'Course we had our differences but think o' what we bin through."

"Yer under arrest," Murphy said evenly. "And I hope they hang ye. Lootin' civilians is punishable by death, though I doubt the court-martial'd consider ye worth th' rope."

"Why, Murphy," the other wheedled, "I was just checking the boy's wagon." He half turned and pointed to the supplies.

Too late for a warning Tim saw Bull draw his pistol and whirl on the unsuspecting sergeant. His quick draw, masked by his body, caught the other by surprise.

"Now, ya black Irishman, let's see ya take me in." Bull held his pistol steady on the sergeant. "Say a prayer," he taunted, "you're not gonna live to report me."

Bull backed away cautiously until he was up against the seat. "Get outa my way, kid," he growled at Tim.

Tim jumped down to the road and moved warily alongside Nellie. He saw Bull's knuckles whiten as the hammer of his pistol moved slowly back. It was clear that Murphy would be dead in a split second.

"Git up, Nellie!" Tim screamed and slapped the flat of his hand against the horse's rump with all his strength. The startled horse lunged forward.

Tim saw Bull grab at the seat for support as the wagon moved out from under him. The seat came loose with a tearing sound as the burly trooper fell off balance.

Murphy vaulted over the wagon side board and grabbed Bull's hand. With a quick twist he sent the pistol flying into the road. Bull kicked out savagely and scrambled to his feet. For a moment the two big troopers traded blows. Murphy moved in, trying to get the trooper into his own powerful hands. The wagon provided an unsteady platform. Tim was having difficulty keeping Nellie quiet.

Murphy drove a short chop to Bull's neck that sent him to his knees. The bed of the wagon was a mess. Corn meal and oats flew under the booted feet of the fighting troopers. Tim saw Bull stagger to his feet, one hand outstretched towards Murphy.

"I've had enough," he gasped.

Murphy dropped his fists and surveyed his corporal with contempt.

With a quick motion Bull swung his other arm and threw a handful of corn meal into Murphy's eyes. As the blinded man fell back, Bull lowered his bullet head and butted the sergeant in the stomach. Murphy's head hit the shattered seat with a sickening thud.

Bull looked around wildly for his pistol. With a bellow of rage, Murphy shook his head and staggered to his feet. Bull jumped out of the wagon and disappeared in the pines. Seconds later Tim heard a horse pound through the trees. He walked back to the wagon to give Murphy a hand.

"Got me horse, th' thievin'——" the sergeant growled as he rubbed the back of his head. He looked around the shambles in the wagon. "Sure an 'tis a mess we've left ye, son." He cocked an eye at the boy. "'Tis thankful I am t' ye, lad, fer yer quick thinkin'. Had ye not startled yer horse, the world'd be less one Irishman." He grinned crookedly. "I'll help ye with the mess, lad." He commenced to straighten the supplies.

Tim scrambled up into the wagon. Suddenly he stood stock-still. When Bull had jerked the seat loose, he had exposed the secret compartment. The three parcels were scattered in plain sight in the wagon bed! Murphy picked one up and stared at it in bewilderment. On its side, in big letters, he could read, "Medical Department."

Murphy looked hard at the boy.

"Where did ye get this?" he demanded.

Tim flushed and swallowed, then set his face stubbornly.

"Speak up! Where did ye get it?"

Tim stared grimly at the trooper but refused to answer.

Murphy turned the parcel over slowly in his hands, then reached out and picked up the other two. He examined them for a long minute. Finally he tucked all three under one arm and jumped down to face the boy.

"Who gave 'em to ye, lad?" he demanded.

Tim stood silent.

Murphy grabbed the boy by the front of his coat. "Ye little fool. D'ye know what ye've done?" He shook Tim until the boy's head snapped back. "D'ye realise ye kin be shot?"

Suddenly the sight of the blue uniform stirred Tim to deep anger. He jerked loose from Murphy's grasp with a savage twist of his body. He faced the sergeant with blazing face and clenched fists. "Go ahead, you damned Yankee! Go ahead and shoot me." Tears of frustration welled up in his eyes. "You've already killed Ma and crippled Pa! Yes, and you burned our home! Why don't you go ahead and shoot me too!"

Murphy stared at the boy for a moment, then slowly turned away.

"All right, lad, take yer horse by the bridle and lead her on to the picket post," he ordered sadly.

Tim did as he was told and silently started Nellie up, Murphy walking behind him alongside the wagon. Tim could hear his big boots every time they hit the hard clay. The Yankee did not say another word. There wasn't anything to say.

CHAPTER FOUR

YANKEES—GOOD AND BAD

"HOLD UP!"

Tim tightened his grip on Nellie's bridle to stop her. The bar across the road was not more than a hundred yards farther on. He saw the picket staring down the road at him and the sergeant.

Murphy walked up from behind the wagon and stood in front of Tim. He took off his cap, scratched his head, and stared at the boy in disgust.

"I'm askin' ye for the last time, boy, where did ye git them medical kits?"

Tim stared sullenly at the ground.

"Speak up, boy! . . . This is your last chance!"

Tim remained stubbornly silent.

Murphy's voice changed to a kinder tone.

"Now look, lad, I know some o' the boys'll sell most anything. Could be your pa's sick and ye had t' have supplies. That's it, ain't it?" he asked eagerly. "One of the orderlies in Fairfax sold ye the stuff."

Tim continued to stare at the ground. He realised Murphy was trying to give him an excuse for having the kits. But suppose he did take a chance and claim he had bought them from some Yankee soldier? . . . Murphy might drag him back to Fairfax to point out the orderly. Once at the headquarters village, someone was sure to remember he had done his business with the sutler, Moore. That would, if not actually lead to Mr.

Moore's arrest, certainly cast suspicion upon him. Tim raised his eyes to meet those of the Irishman. He did not say anything; he just stared at the big soldier unafraid. Murphy returned the boy's stare. Tim knew that the big man realised the truth. Murphy finally looked away and stared up ahead to the road-block. To Tim it seemed ages before he spoke again.

"When ye git past that log up yonder," the Irishman said quietly, "don't ever come back." He shook his big head slowly. "No Murphy ain't ever fought kids before and this one ain't gonna start it now." He turned to face the boy again. "Ye've had it tough, lad, no doubt, but war ain't fun for anyone. The innocent's like to get hurt with the rest." His face turned grim again. "But mind this, lad, don't ye ever, hear me, ever, come this way again!"

Murphy turned away and headed on up the road. He threw a "Come on," over his shoulder, not bothering to see whether Tim started out or not.

Tim clucked quietly to Nellie, and the old horse leaned forward in the traces to get the wagon started. Once again the boy started walking, his eyes on the broad blue back just ahead. He wrestled with his thoughts. He wanted to hate that uniform and everything it stood for, yet he just could not find it in his heart to hate Murphy. He knew he should be relieved that the sergeant was going to let him go, but somehow he felt like a little boy caught cheating. If he were a little bigger, maybe Murphy would have tried to beat an answer out of him. Tim wished he were bigger; somehow he did not want to be let go scot free. He wanted to fight the Irishman for his freedom.

A few paces before the swinging log, Murphy raised his arm and motioned the guard to clear the road. Tim did not even have to slow Nellie down. He nodded to the trooper at the road-block and continued on his way. Behind him he heard Murphy say to the trooper, "I found these medical kits down the road. Send 'em back to Fairfax with the next soldier who goes to town."

Tim looked over his shoulder for a last glance at the outpost. Murphy, walking slowly to the little cluster of tents, was not even watching the road. The trooper noticed the boy look back and he waved. Tim raised his hand slowly in reply, then turned to the road. He realised this was probably the last time he would be driving this way for a long time, at least until the Yankees were pushed back north. He knew Murphy meant he was not to come back. Next time the big sergeant would arrest him.

Tim wondered what Captain Mosby would think of the incident. Now he could not do any more under-cover work. All Pa's planning for a way to help was of no avail. Tim knew he should feel bad but somehow he felt relieved. His job had been much too sneaky, even if it did help the South. Suddenly a thought crossed his mind. If he couldn't be an undercover agent, maybe the Captain would now let him join the Rangers for good! With the thought his spirits soared.

"Git up, Nellie, old gal. Let's git home!" He straightened his shoulders. Trooper Morgan! By golly, that sounded good!

Nellie seemed to sense the change in her driver's spirits. She picked up the pace a bit and looked almost sprightly.

With the thought of possible action with the Rangers to keep him company, Tim found his wagon rumbling over the wooden bridge across Cub Run before he realised it. He pulled Nellie into the trail through the forest and listened for Prince's bark. As the wagon bumped over the rutted road, he became uneasy, because he heard no sound from his dog. Prince never failed to signal any approach along the trail. True, the dog might be in the cabin, but Tim doubted it. Pa didn't hold with dogs being inside in good weather.

Suddenly the wagon broke out of the woods into the clearing. Tim's heart leaped. Just in front of the cabin door he saw the prone figure of his father on the ground.

"Git up, Nellie!" he screamed and slapped the reins against the startled mare's flanks. Nellie broke into a gallop, dragging the bouncing wagon behind her.

Tim hit the dirt on a dead run long before the old horse came to a tottering halt. He ran to where his father lay face down.

"Pa! Pa!" he yelled. "What's the matter, Pa?"

Gently he rolled his father over, and to his horror saw that one side of his face was streaked with blood. Carefully he straightened the unconscious man and felt tenderly in the matted hair. When his fingers touched an open wound, his father groaned.

"Easy, Pa," cautioned Tim. He ran into the house, grabbed a basin of water from the sideboard, a cloth from alongside the fireplace, then dashed back outside. Carefully he bathed his father's bloodstained face and matted hair. While ugly, the wound did not seem deep. Tim saw his father's eyes flutter, then open. The older man tried to sit up.

"Easy, Pa," said the boy, afraid the wound might start bleeding again.

"I'm all right, I guess, Tim," said his father.

Suddenly his eyes and manner grew alert. "Get inside quick, Tim, and get the pistol. Hurry now!" he added urgently.

Once again Tim ran into the house, cleared away the dirt over the secret hiding place, opened the black box, and lifted the Colt revolver. He spun the cylinder quickly to make sure it was loaded, then ran back outside. His father was sitting up now, his eyes warily scanning the circling forest. He took the pistol from Tim's hand as the boy ran up, then drew him down to the ground.

"Keep your eye on the woods while we talk, Tim," he warned. "Your eyes are probably better than mine right now; I'm still a mite dizzy."

"Who was it, Pa?" asked Tim anxiously. "What happened?"

Never once taking his eyes from the woods, Tim's father told him of his accident. "I heard Prince bark," he explained, "and went to the cabin door. There was a Yankee ridin' into the clearin'. I figgered him to be an advance scout of some foragin' party, so I waited for him to ride up." Tim's father winced as he shifted his body. "This Yank rode up with a pistol in his hand and ordered me away from the door. Said he was supposed to requisition food for the army. Wasn't much I could do except let him in the cabin."

"Did any more Yankees follow him?" asked Tim anxiously, as his eyes scanned the forest.

"No, he was alone," answered his father. "He ordered me to fill a gunny sack with food. I began to get suspicious—the way he was acting—and started askin' questions. I could tell he was in a real big hurry. When we went back outside, Prince was carryin' on, barking and growling. The Yankee kicked at him. Prince broke his rope and started after him. I tried to grab the dog, but before I could, the devil shot him."

Tim looked over to where the dog lay silent on the ground. Tears of rage welled up in his eyes.

"Then," his father continued, "I guess I lost my head. In the confusion I made a grab for the Yankee." The older man felt his wound gingerly. "I missed," he exclaimed ruefully. "The last thing I remember was about a million bright lights." He started to get to his feet, but fell back with a groan.

"Sit still, Pa!" cried Tim. "Let me get a bandage on your head, then we'll go over to the Carter place. Missus Carter'll know what to do."

"I'll be all right in a minute," said his father. "Only grazed me, I reckon."

Tim didn't say anything for a minute, then he asked quietly, "What did the Yankee look like, Pa?"

The father glanced at his son sharply. "He was a big man, as big as me . . . one of the 5th New York. Leastwise he wore their insignia." His father thought for a minute. "Had a scar, a long one, running down his right cheekbone."

Tim nodded quietly. "That was Bull Ruffing, Pa."

His father's eyes widened in amazement. "You mean that Yankee who stopped you on the turnpike?"

"Yes, sir, the same."

Minutely Tim related the story of Murphy's fight with Bull and the Yankee's subsequent desertion.

For a moment, Tim's father sat silent.

"You're a lucky boy, Tim," he finally said. "And I'm lucky not to have lost you." He glanced fondly at his son. "In a way, I'm glad this undercover work is over, too. We have to get word to Mosby, and let Moore know. His job in Fairfax is too risky now. He'll have to go some place else for a while."

"That's the way I figger it, Pa," said Tim. "First let me get you over to Missus Carter. She'll take care of your head like it oughta be taken care of. I can cut through the woods to Fairfax and warn Mr. Moore."

"No!" exclaimed his father sharply. "I can't let you go back to Fairfax. We'll get word to Moore some other way."

"But, Pa——"

"No buts about it. Murphy might be in town. He gave you fair warning. You can't expect him to let you off again."

Tim noticed that the newly applied bandage on his father's head had begun to redden around the wound.

"We better get over to the Carter place, Pa."

His father raised a hand to the bandage and said, "Head wounds always bleed a lot." He got to his feet unsteadily, tried to stand alone. He swayed uncertainly until Tim threw a strong young arm around his waist.

"Pa, you ought to rest a while!" exclaimed Tim in alarm.

"I'll be all right," answered his father. "We'll take the wagon over to the Carter place."

Tim led his father to a bench alongside the cabin door and made him sit down. He ran inside rolled up the feather mattress from his bed and carried it to the back of the wagon. A few more trips and he had most of the things they would need for a few days away from home; he figured they would be gone at least until Mosby could be found and until his father had a complete rest. The last thing he did in the cabin was to remove the paper which Mosby had given him, confirming his status as a trooper in the Partisan band. He covered the place of concealment carefully. No telling when the secret compartment might be needed in the future.

Outside again, he noticed how pale and drawn his father's face appeared. Alarmed, Tim tried to hurry the older man into the wagon.

"Let's go, Pa," he said anxiously. "You can lay on the mattress and the ridin' won't be so rough."

He glanced around the now-darkening clearing, saw Prince, and with a tug of regret wished that he had had time to bury the faithful dog. His father had the same thought. "Get the pick and shovel, Tim. Least we can do for a good friend is give him a decent burial," he said.

"We don't have time, Pa."

"Yes, we do," answered the father firmly. "Hurry now and get the tools."

Tim chose a spot near the corner of the cabin and dug a shallow grave. Tenderly he lifted the dog into the opening, and, almost blinded by tears, hastily shovelled the earth into the hole. He tramped the earth down, then hurried back to help his father into the wagon.

With darkness a slight drizzle began. Anxious for his father's comfort, Tim spread a waterproof over him and tried to keep Nellie on firm ground as he drove along the pitch-black road. The thought kept running through his mind that Bull Ruffing lurked somewhere in the woods. His hand strayed often to the handle of the Colt he had strapped around his waist. Of one thing he was sure, if Ruffing did try to stop him, he'd fight his way through.

Although the Carter farmhouse lay but three miles west of the cabin, the trip seemed to take ages. When he finally did arrive at the turn-off leading to the house, he probably would have missed it in the darkness had not the Carter dogs set up a noisy fuss. The house was shrouded in darkness, for few families kept their lanterns lighted in these troubled times. Not until he drove the wagon abreast of the porch did a light appear in one of the downstairs rooms. He heard a window open.

"Who's there?" came a woman's voice. "Make yourself known or I'll turn the dogs loose."

Tim caught the glint of light on steel and reckoned Missus Carter had a shotgun pointed at them.

"It's me, Tim Morgan, Missus Carter!" he yelled.

Tim could not stop pacing the floor. His father looked white and drawn as he lay on the best settee in Mrs. Carter's living room, but if anyone could help, certainly Mrs. Carter could. She had cared for the folks all over the country these many years and often took care of any stray wounded Confederates in the vicinity. He remembered hearing his father say she had saved more of Mosby's Rangers than the army doctors.

After what seemed hours, the woman finally finished her examination of the wound and straightened up.

"Ben Morgan," she said, shaking her head. "You're about the luckiest man I know. If that bullet had been a mite more to the left, Tim could have left you at home —under the sod." She looked at him with mock severity. "Not that you're in right good shape even now. You've lost a lot of blood and you're going to need plenty of rest." She turned to Tim. "You can stop pacin' now and we'll get your pa up to a bedroom. He'll rest easier where he can stretch out."

There was no question in Tim's mind but that his father looked a great deal more comfortable in the big four-poster bed. It didn't take Ben Morgan long to drop off into an exhausted sleep soon after Mrs. Carter put a clean bandage on the wound.

Tim had intended to sit by his father's bedside for a while, but when Mrs. Carter picked up the lamp and started out of the room she beckoned to him.

"No need for you to sit up here, Tim," she said. "Your pa will sleep for hours. You come with me, I want to talk with you."

Tim followed her downstairs to the kitchen. Once there, she cut him a generous portion of apple pie, a treat he hadn't tasted for months.

"Eat that first, then tell me what happened."

Between bites Tim told her he had made a trip to Fairfax and on his return found his father wounded. He told her that the assailant was undoubtedly a Union deserter. He omitted the reason for his trip. After the sketchy account, he could see she guessed there was more to the story.

Mrs. Carter studied the boy for a moment.

"I don't know what you Morgans are up to, living in that cabin down there on Cub Run," she held up her hand as Tim looked up, "and I don't want to. Whatever you're doing is your own business."

Tim didn't say anything for a minute. He almost told her of his activities for Mosby, then decided there was no point in involving any more people.

"I don't think we'll be going back, Missus Carter," he said. "I don't know exactly what Pa will do."

"What are your plans, young man?"

"Soon as Pa's all right, I'm going to join up with Mosby, ma'am."

Mrs. Carter sniffed. "Nonsense, Tim! You're too young. Let them as has their growth do the fighting."

"I'm almost sixteen, ma'am," said Tim defensively. "Captain Mosby said he'd take me when—when I reached sixteen," he added.

"Well, then he's a fool. John Mosby ought to have better sense." Mrs. Carter reached over and placed a hand on Tim's arm. "There now, Tim, I know how you boys want to do your part. I guess I'm foolish, but it breaks my heart to see all you youngsters going into the army."

"But, ma'am, we've got to drive the Yankees out of Virginia."

"I know, I know," said the woman sadly. "We have the right on our side, but that doesn't make the war any easier to endure."

"It won't last much longer, Missus Carter. General Lee'll drive the Yankees clear to New York by the end of summer."

Mrs. Carter smiled thinly. "There are those who said the war wouldn't last three months, Tim. That was a year ago," she reminded him gently. Suddenly she stood up. "But enough of this. Go put Nellie in the barn, then get to bed."

"Yes, ma'am," said Tim. "I'll take a look around outside."

Mrs. Carter glanced at him sharply. "You don't think that deserter might come around here, do you?"

"No, ma'am. I'm sure he won't," answered Tim with more conviction than he felt.

"If he does, the dogs'll let us know well ahead of time." she promised. "Between my shotgun and your pistol we'll give him a warm reception," she added grimly.

Tim watered and fed Nellie and rubbed her down thoroughly. The old mare had been through a busy day. Tim spoke to her soothingly, and stroked her nose. Thank heaven, he thought, she's too old for the Yankees to take. The mere thought of Yankees started him wondering where Bull might have gone. While he didn't want to worry Mrs. Carter, he was sure the Yankee deserter would pick on lonely farms until he could get clear of both armies. Although Tim had no idea what Ruffing planned to do, he imagined he would want to get north as quickly as possible and lose himself in one of the large cities. Before he left for the north, undoubtedly he would steal anything he could. Tim decided he'd better look around outside. He blew out the oil lamp he'd carried into the barn and went out into the black night.

For several minutes Tim stood motionless and listened. Except for an occasional night bird and a few crickets, all was quiet; dark too, he realised, as he looked vainly for stars overhead. He circled the barn slowly, stopping occasionally to listen, then made his way to the rear of the house. Mrs. Carter had two dogs, one chained at the front of the house and one at the rear. He spoke quietly to the latter as he approached. The dog whined and Tim patted its head. He moved around to the front and spoke quietly to the second hound. Both dogs were alert, and he was sure that no one could approach the house without their setting up a fuss. Convinced he would have warning if Bull Ruffing did try to sneak up on them, he re-entered the house. Mrs. Carter was still in the kitchen.

"You look ready to fall in your tracks, boy," she said. "Why don't you go to bed?"

"Yes, ma'am, I will," he answered. Then, hesitating only briefly, he continued, "You think Pa's going to be all right?"

"Land sakes, Tim," she exclaimed. "Of course he is. I told you he'd be right as rain when he gets his strength back." She eyed him curiously. "Now what's on your mind, young man?"

"Well—the truth is, ma'am, I have to see Captain Mosby about something mighty important."

" 'Mighty important' like, 'Will he take you in the army?' " she chided him.

"No, ma'am," said Tim seriously. "This is real important and I oughta get to him as quick as I can."

"Does this have something to do with why you and your pa were living down on Cub Run?"

"Yes, ma'am."

"Well, then," said Mrs. Carter quietly, "you better get to him. But you can't leave to-night. Get some rest and leave early in the morning. Don't worry about your pa. He can stay here as long as he wants. The good Lord knows there's enough needs fixin' around this farm, and when your pa's up and about again, he can tend to it." She put her arm around the boy's shoulder. "Now you get to bed and we'll talk to your pa in the morning. Get along now."

The next morning Ben Morgan left no doubt in Mrs. Carter's mind that Tim must find Mosby. Although he did not tell her the reason, he realised that the Partisan leader had to get word to the sutler Moore, who might be under suspicion. Even though Tim and his father believed Murphy would say nothing about the medical supplies to his officers, there was always a chance he might do some checking on his next trip to Fairfax. Moore should be warned to shift his field of operations. Tim was to tell Mosby that Ben Morgan would remain at the Carter farm until he heard from the Ranger chief.

At length Tim broached the question uppermost in his mind: "What if the Captain lets me join up, Pa? I can't do anything more here."

Ben Morgan looked at his son. He knew that Tim would never be happy until he was in the army. He remembered also his tacit approval of Tim's request the night Mosby had come to their cabin.

"You've pretty much reached your own decision, son," he said. "I won't stand in your way. You're a man now, or almost, and I'm sure you can handle yourself like one."

"Ben Morgan!" protested Mrs. Carter, who had remained silent as long as she could. "This boy is much too young!"

Tim's father shook his head slowly. "No one's really too young to do his part. What you don't know is that Tim has already been doing a man's work for the South."

"Will you be all right here?" Tim asked his father.

"Of course, I'll be all right," said Ben Morgan. "In a day or two I'll be up taking care of the barn door and the south fence and all the other things that need tendin' to."

" 'Deed you won't, Ben Morgan," said Mrs. Carter. "You'll stay in bed 'til I think you're well enough to get up, and that's that," she added with finality.

Ben Morgan winked at his son. "You better get on your way, Tim, or she might decide to keep you around here too."

"For once I agree with your father," said Mrs. Carter. "If you're bound to go you'd best get on your way. I'll pack you some food. With all the gallivantin' around John Mosby does, it's hard to tell when you'll meet up with him."

When Mrs. Carter left the room, Tim's father motioned him to move closer to the bed.

"Mosby's not that hard to find," he said in a low voice. "Head west on the turnpike until you pass the Walkers' place. About a mile beyond you'll be stopped.

Could be it'll be a farmer in a wagon, or maybe a mounted man. The turnpike's always watched along there. No one goes by without Mosby knowing who they are and why they're on the move. Just tell whoever stops you that you want to see the Captain. They'll get you to him."

"Suppose I see Yankees on the road?"

"Don't bother with them, and I don't think they'll bother you. They're not likely to stop a boy just riding alone on the turnpike."

"You think I ought to take Nellie?" asked Tim.

"Of course," replied his father. "She's old and she's slow, but she'll get you there. You can bring or send her back later."

"Then I guess I'd better get on my way," said Tim reluctantly. Anxious as he was to contact Mosby, he still did not like his father's looks. Tim wondered whether Mrs. Carter was right, or was the wound perhaps more serious than she thought.

His father held out his hand.

"Be careful, son."

"I will, Pa," said Tim clasping the hand firmly. He turned and left the bedside before his father could see the tell-tale glistening in his eyes.

Mrs. Carter had a burlap bag ready for him. There seemed to be enough food in it for a week.

"You don't know how long it will take you to find John Mosby," she said when he protested.

He hoisted the bag over his shoulder and moved to the back door.

"Thanks, Missus Carter. I'll be back to see you and Pa first chance I get."

"No thanks needed, Tim," said the woman kindly. "Don't fret about your pa and for goodness sake, be careful."

Tim nodded and went out into the yard. He stopped for a moment to pat Mrs. Carter's hound, and the picture of Prince, jumping for joy on the end of his leash, flashed across his mind. He straightened his shoulders and walked on to the barn. Bull Ruffing would pay, he told himself, if he ever met the brute again.

Little River Turnpike was quiet in the early morning. No one had passed the boy in three hours since he had left the farm. Folks were mighty chary of using the road these days. If Yankee patrols weren't clattering down its rutted surface, Confederate scouting parties were. Peaceful folk stayed home rather than take a chance on losing what little they still possessed. Although the road was deserted, Tim rode cautiously, with many a look at the woods on either side. It would be like Ruffing to watch the road for any unwary single traveller. With this thought in mind, Tim's hand continually strayed to the grip of his Colt.

At noon-time he pulled Nellie off the road into the woods, found a small stream, and sat down beside it to eat his lunch. Just as he finished he heard the muted sound of horses on the turnpike. He crept through the woods and hid in the underbrush alongside the road. Within minutes he saw a platoon of Yankee cavalry go by at a trot. After they had passed, he returned to the stream and waited a while before setting out again. No sense inviting danger by following too close on their heels.

By late afternoon Tim had passed the Walker farm. He did not go up to the house, but rode on, eager to make contact with Mosby's men.

About two miles beyond the farm Tim saw a single horseman approaching him slowly. As he drew nearer, he could see that the other traveller was dressed completely in black and rode a mule. The man was long, lean, and lantern-jawed. As Tim rode up, he stopped the mule and waited. Cradled in one arm he held a well-worn Bible.

"Good day to you, young man," he said and raised his hat politely.

"Good day, sir," said Tim and started on past. Obviously the man was an itinerant preacher, several of whom roved the country, preaching to the mountain folk farther west.

"Surely, my boy, you can't be in a hurry on such a fine day." He raised a long, bony hand towards the sky. "The Lord in His kindness has provided us with weather too balmy to waste in haste." He stared at the boy with dark, piercing eyes.

Tim, not wanting to seem rude, stopped Nellie again. "It sure is a beautiful day. That's a fact," said Tim.

The preacher opened his Bible.

"Let me send you on your way, young man, with a thought from the Good Book." He opened the Bible and slowly thumbed through the pages. Finally, after locating the right verse, he nudged his mule up alongside Nellie.

Suddenly a long arm shot out and Tim's pistol was in the man's hand.

"And now, my boy," said the other, "just where are

you going? What's your name, and why are you wearing a fine Colt revolver?"

Tim was so surprised that he could do nothing but stare into the piercing eyes for a full minute.

"I'm waiting," said the man coldly.

It crossed Tim's mind that the garb of a preacher would be an excellent cover for a Yankee spy. On the other hand, the man might be a common thief masquerading as a preacher. He thought quickly.

"I'm on my way to Aldie," he said, naming the nearest town, "and that gun is one Pa gave me. Guess he found it."

The man looked the gun over carefully.

"This is a Yankee gun, and a new one," said the man accusingly. He stared at the boy suspiciously, then whistled sharply.

Two men on horseback broke out of the woods some distance up the road and came galloping towards them.

"What's up, Jeptha?" asked one as they looked the boy over carefully.

"He has a mighty thin story," said the man on the mule. "Mighty thin."

Tim saw that each horseman wore two pistols, and in their saddle holsters each carried a rifle. Then for the first time he noticed their hats were pinned up on one side. A tiny feather stuck out of the pin. He grinned in relief.

"I'm looking for Captain Mosby," he said boldly.

The three men looked at each other in surprise. Finally one of the horsemen took Tim's pistol from the preacher and shoved it in his belt.

"You'll see him all right," he said coldly.

CHAPTER FIVE

THE TAMING OF A SHREW

THE FIRST thing Tim noticed in the dimly lit barn that Mosby used for headquarters was the fire in the middle of the floor. Whoever laid that fire knew what he was doing. Though practically no smoke rose from the glowing coals, Tim could feel the warmth as he stepped inside. Someone had driven a pair of stakes into the earth floor, and from a cross bar between the two had hung a large coffee pot. His eyes, accustomed to the darkness outside, permitted a quick assessment of the contents of the barn.

Only two men sat near the fire; there were others in several of the hay-filled stalls, and a glance at the loft showed booted feet sticking over the edge of the supporting beam. One thing struck Tim forcibly: where-ever there was a trooper sprawled in the hay, close at hand was a gun belt with guns, sabre, and rifle. From one of the stalls a grey horse looked Tim over, then stamped impatiently and tossed its head.

In the far corner of the structure a slight man in cadet grey sat at a field table where an oil lamp cast a small circle of light. Tim could not make out the face in the shadows above the circle of light, but he did recognise the cape when he caught a gleam of red as the man shifted his position. This was Mosby!

"Move along, sonny!" Tim's guard nudged him in the back and gestured towards the field table.

Tim moved forward, the trooper right behind him. He circled the fire and walked up to within a pace or two of Mosby.

For several minutes, it seemed to Tim, Mosby kept his eyes glued on what was apparently a map. Finally he looked up.

"Yes?"

There were no signs of recognition in the Partisan's eyes.

"Found this boy on the turnpike, sir," Tim's guard answered. "Says he knows you, sir. Claims his name's Morgan."

Mosby leaned forward, picked up the lamp, and held it close to Tim's face. Satisfied, he spoke to the guard.

"Thanks, Sam, I'll take care of the lad. He's Morgan all right."

As the trooper turned and started across the barn, Mosby motioned to a keg resting on one side of the table.

"Sit down, Tim," he said in a kindly voice. "What can we do for you?"

Tim's long pent-up emotions were released. He began to tell his story. Except for an occasional nod, the Confederate officer let the boy get everything out of his system. When Tim had finished, Mosby stared at him intently.

"You say your father is not seriously wounded."

"No, sir—at least Missus Carter said the bullet just grazed Pa's head." Tim shook his head slowly. "I can't rightly say, sir. Pa lost an awful lot of blood and sure was weak and sick lookin'."

Mosby placed his hand on Tim's shoulder. "We'll

take care of him, Tim. Don't fret. We'll also take care of this Ruffing." He fell silent for a minute, then looked Tim over from head to foot.

The boy became acutely conscious of his worn clothes and old boots. He could not help comparing his own appearance with the fastidious Ranger captain, whose shiny black boots showed not a speck of dust. Tim looked up from his scrutiny to find Mosby staring at him.

"And what are your plans, Tim?"

Tim stood up quickly, unbuttoned his shirt and pulled out the paper that Mosby had written that night at the cabin. He handed it to the Captain.

"I'd like to report for duty, sir," he said stiffly.

Mosby glanced at the paper, then stood up and faced the boy. Actually shorter and lighter in weight than young Morgan, Mosby seemed big because of the erect carriage he maintained at all times.

"Does your father know of your intentions, Tim?" Mosby eyed the boy searchingly.

"Yes, sir."

"Are you sure you wouldn't rather go into one of the regular regiments?" Mosby asked. "I feel certain that General Stuart would find you a place in the cavalry."

"No, sir!" Tim replied, alarmed at the suggestion that he ride with any other command.

Mosby smiled faintly at Tim's vehemence, then quickly sobered.

"You understand that all of my men are veteran troopers, Tim. All have had battle experience before they joined me."

Tim began to get really alarmed now. It sounded as if

Captain Mosby was trying to let him down easy. It had never occurred to him that he might have to serve in the regular army.

"But, sir," Tim protested. "I can ride and shoot. Pa says I'm a real good shot, sir." He ran a hand through his thick mop of hair. "As far as the experience is concerned, I can get it with your Rangers."

Mosby shook his head slowly. "That might prove fatal, son."

Tim stared at the Ranger captain. "But, sir, I thought I was already a part of your command. You said all I needed on that paper was a date."

"That's right, Tim, and it still holds. All I'm saying is that you cannot raid with my men until I know you're ready."

Tim waited expectantly.

"You'll have to prove to me you are ready," Mosby continued. "Starting to-morrow morning one of my men will take you in hand. Pay close attention to all he tells you, and you'll learn a trooper's duties."

"Yes, sir!" replied Tim eagerly.

Mosby sat down at the table again, picked up a pen, and with a flourish wrote in a date on the paper.

"Now you are a trooper," he said, "but remember, Tim, our Rangers' success depends on several facts. Rangers are first of all good cavalrymen. While they obey orders instantly, they also have to think fast in an emergency, and above all, success depends on the element of surprise."

"Yes, sir!" replied Tim, his eyes on the paper that now proclaimed him a trooper.

Mosby stood up abruptly. "Slaughter!" he called.

A lean, wiry man sitting near the fire rose from his place and joined the two at the table.

"Yes, sir," the trooper reported.

Tim looked the man over and thought with a feeling of complacency that here was another trooper not much heftier than himself. . . . But he envied the man's easy composure as he stood waiting before the Captain. His uniform showed signs of wear, and Tim noticed that he wore two guns even though the others in the barn had taken theirs off.

"Morgan here has joined our command, Sergeant," said Mosby. "Please have him outfitted." He turned to Tim. "Do you need a horse, Morgan?"

Tim hesitated for a moment. "I—I rode Nellie here, sir. I reckon Pa'll be needin' her for the ploughin' if . . ."

"Let him have a pick of that bunch we brought in last night, Sergeant." Mosby's eyes showed his amusement. "I think perhaps Nellie deserves lighter duty than she will get here."

Tim grinned. "Yes, sir!"

"You can take her back in a few days."

"Thank you, sir," replied Tim.

Mosby turned back to his map, but as Tim started to move away with Slaughter, the Captain spoke again.

"You say your father is at the Carter place?"

"Yes, sir," answered Tim, and with the question he remembered his father's condition. By rights he should ask permission to go back to see how Pa was.

"Don't worry about your father. We'll see to him," said Mosby as if anticipating the boy's request. "Go along now and get outfitted."

Slaughter led Tim to the far end of the barn where a pile of clothing lay in a heap on the floor. The sergeant looked the boy over critically for a moment, then dug a pair of trousers and a jacket out of the pile and handed them over.

Tim judged that the uniform would fit even before he slipped out of his old clothes and put it on. He was not wrong. Both trousers and jacket fitted perfectly. As he buttoned up the coat, he noticed that the fine wool cloth was practically new. Except for a small hole in the left breast, which had been neatly mended, it was in perfect condition. He ran his forefinger over the small hole and realised that no one would notice it unless he looked very closely.

"These fit fine, sir," said Tim proudly. "How come such a fine uniform doesn't belong to someone?"

Slaughter spoke to the boy for the first time. "Don't call me 'sir.' I ain't no officer—and besides, the feller that owned 'em don't need 'em any more."

Tim looked down at his finger still caressing the small hole in the jacket, then hastily pulled his hand away.

"I see, s—I see," he said thoughtfully.

"You got any guns?" Slaughter asked abruptly.

"Yes," said Tim.

"Reckon you'll need a sabre." The sergeant selected one from several hanging in scabbards along the wall. "This oughta fit. Put it on."

Tim buckled the sabre belt around his waist. Unaccustomed to its weight, it was uncomfortable hanging along his leg.

Slaughter shoved a hat at him.

"Fits fine," said Tim when he had put it on at a jaunty angle.

The sergeant then pointed to a pile of boots.

Tim dropped to his knees and went through them carefully. There were all types of boots piled up in the heap. He found one boot of fine English leather that looked about his size. He tried it on. He had not realised that there were such boots in existence. The leather fitted his foot like a comfortable glove. He hurriedly searched the pile for its mate, fearful lest it not be there. When he did find it, he slipped it on and stood up.

"Can I have these?" he asked.

"If they fit," answered Slaughter. "You're lucky. Been a dozen fellers tried them boots on. You're the first that looked like he could walk in 'em."

"They sure are fine boots," said Tim admiringly.

"Belonged to an English duke or lord who rode with us a spell," offered Slaughter. "Funny thing," he mused, "he sure could ride, but he warn't much shakes at duckin'."

Tim looked down at the boots again. There was one thing sure about his outfit, he thought: there would be no former owners to dispute his claim. He walked back and forth, unconsciously strutting just a bit. The heavy sabre clanked at his side as it banged against his leg. He wondered whether he would ever get accustomed to the irritating feel of it.

"Better bed down now," said Slaughter. "There's straw in the stables. Pick an oilskin off the pegs over there." He pointed to a group of shiny black rain cloaks hanging against the wall.

Tim chose a raincoat, gathered an armful of hay from the nearest stable, and prepared a bed on the floor. Just as he started to lie down, he saw a bearded man enter the barn and go to Mosby's table. After a few quiet words, this man called softly to two others who rose at once and left with him.

Someone going on a scout, thought Tim. Suddenly he was overcome with weariness. The minute his head hit the straw he was sound asleep.

In about five minutes, or so it seemed to Tim, he was awakened by someone nudging him with his toe. He rubbed his eyes sleepily, sat up, and saw Slaughter standing over him.

"If you don't eat now, you might not get any," said the sergeant.

Tim glanced towards the fire and saw at least two dozen men sitting there on their haunches, busily engaged in stowing away as much breakfast as they could. He jumped up quickly and reached for his sabre.

"You won't need that to cut your bacon," said the sergeant in amusement. "Grab a plate. The cook'll fill it."

Tim moved elf-consciously towards the circle of men, feeling strange among these veteran troopers, but except for a casual glance from one or two, no one seemed a bit interested in him. He took a tin plate from a pile on the floor and held it out to an older trooper who was obviously the cook. The man piled on a generous helping of bacon and two huge slabs of corn bread, then handed Tim a cup of steaming coffee.

"Reckon that'll hold ye, sonny?" The cook's lips

parted in a broken-toothed grin. "Iffen it won't, there's plenty more," he added.

Tim mumbled his thanks, then found a place to eat away from the fire. He was ravenous, and within a few minutes had cleaned the plate. He looked up to see the other troopers filing out of the barn. In the far corner, he saw Captain Mosby still busy at the field table. He wondered whether the man ever slept. Further thoughts about the subject were interrupted by Sergeant Slaughter, who beckoned to him. Tim rose hastily, dumped his plate and cup into a tub of steaming water, as he had seen the others do, and hurried towards the sergeant.

"Get your gear and follow me," ordered the man.

Tim ran back to his makeshift bed, folded his oilskin, strapped on his sabre and guns, and returned. Without another word Slaughter turned and left the barn, Tim trailing along behind him.

Once outside, Tim saw it was still fairly dark although a few streaks of light spread across the eastern sky. The other troopers were mounting up, and the boy looked questioningly at his guide.

"Not you and me," he said. "We got work to do."

At that moment, Mosby came out into the barnyard, accompanied by the same black-bearded man Tim had seen come and go the night before. Mosby swept by, walking directly to a magnificent grey held by a trooper. His companion stopped and looked at Tim with the kindest eyes the boy had ever seen.

"You're young Morgan?"

Tim glanced at the bars on the man's coat and said, "Yes, sir."

"I'm Doctor Dunn." The man held out his hand. "I looked at your father last night. We had an interesting hour together. He'll be all right. He sends you his best and tells you to obey your commander."

"Thank you, sir," Tim said gratefully. "And I will, sir."

"I'm sure you will," said the doctor with a smile. He glanced at Sergeant Slaughter. "I leave you in good hands." He winked at the sergeant, then hurried on to his waiting mount.

Tim looked after the full-bearded doctor with a new warmth in his heart. Mosby meant what he said when he promised they would look after Pa. The Captain must have sent the doctor and the two troopers all the way to the Carter place just to check on Pa's condition. He watched with pride as the wiry little captain looked over his small band, raised a white-gloved hand, then galloped out of the barnyard.

"We better pick you a horse," said Slaughter over his shoulder, and headed around the barn. He went to a line of picketed mounts tethered to a long rope strung between two upright posts.

Tim's heart leaped when he saw Nellie grazing calmly among the well-fed cavalry mounts. He ran to her and rubbed her nose gently. The old mare nuzzled the boy's cheek.

"Here, give her this," said the sergeant with some embarrassment as he handed Tim a chunk of brown sugar.

Tim let Nellie take the sugar from his open palm, and he stroked her head as she savoured the sweet.

"Come on, come on. Let's get movin'," said

Slaughter with a show of brusqueness. "We can't waste half the day gettin' a horse for ya."

Tim gave Nellie a pat and backed off to look over the string of mounts. Slaughter did not fool him. No matter how harsh he sounded, the sergeant liked horses, and Tim knew they would get along. He let his eyes move up and down the line. Suddenly he spotted a small black tethered between two chestnuts. Her ears were pointed and her head turned towards him. Tim moved closer and looked the horse over critically in the growing light.

"Like that mare?" asked the sergeant.

"She sure is a pretty thing," said Tim approvingly. The mare was completely black, except for a small white blaze on her forehead. He reached forward tentatively to stroke her nose. The mare snapped her head high, her eyes rolling white in fear.

"Touchy," mused the trooper.

"She don't know me yet," answered Tim confidently. "Do you have another chunk of that sugar, Mr. Slaughter?"

The sergeant handed Tim another small piece of sugar and Tim held it on the palm of his hand and moved forward very slowly. The mare rolled her eyes again, watching the hand warily. Suddenly her head darted forward, her teeth snapping viciously. Tim jumped back and narrowly missed losing a finger.

"Ain't the friendly type, is she, boy?"

"She's just scared," answered Tim. "Reckon I'll have to show her I'm not going to hurt her." He moved down the line to where Nellie stood patiently, untethered the old horse, then led her up alongside the black. Careful to keep the older mare between himself and the younger, he tied Nellie alongside the frisky mount. He stroked his horse's nose gently, murmuring in her ear. Out of the corner of his eye he could see the black watching him curiously. Tim broke the sugar in half and let Nellie take it from his hand. Patiently he waited for her to roll it around in her mouth and swallow it. Slowly he advanced his open hand with the other half towards the black. The young mare eyed it nervously, eased her head forward, and took the sugar from the boy's hand with a quick smack of her lips.

Tim grinned and stroked Nellie's nose again. "Tell her I won't hurt her, old girl," he said softly. "Tell her I like horses."

Suddenly the black seemed to lose interest in the boy. She dropped her head and commenced quietly to munch the grass.

"That's a trained Yankee horse," said Slaughter. "Let's get a saddle on her and see what she's like."

The black stood quietly when the sergeant threw a saddle on her back. Tim held her head while the older man tightened the girth and stepped back.

"She's all yours, son."

Tim moved slowly to the black's side. Although the mare was well trained, she seemed to be a one-man mount. He believed that if he could once straddle her he could master her. Cautiously he placed one foot in the stirrup, then swung into the saddle.

The mare stood still momentarily. Tim could feel her quiver.

Suddenly she bolted, head down, and Tim was powerless to drag her head up. She ran to the nearest fence and stopped abruptly, head still down low. Tim went flying over the mare's head, landed rolling in the dust, and came up against the fence with a violent thump. He got up slowly and looked down at his uniform. He brushed the dust off as best he could and looked the now quiet mare in the eye.

"All right, young lady. You just wait right here. I'll be back," he said grimly.

He limped across the yard towards the barn.

"Where you goin', sonny?" asked the sergeant, unable to conceal his amusement.

"I'll be right back," Tim called over his shoulder and continued on to the barn.

Within a few minutes the young trooper was back, this time dressed in his old clothes of the night before. Several of the troopers who had remained at the barn sauntered over to see the fun.

"I ain't sure she likes you, trooper," said Slaughter when Tim walked up to the mare again.

"She will," said Tim determinedly.

He picked up the reins again and eased up alongside the black.

"Whoa, now," he soothed as he placed his foot in the stirrup. Quickly he swung into the saddle.

This time the black moved as Tim hit the saddle. She bolted forward, then pivoted before the boy could get set. The quick motion threw him a second time. Tim sat in the dust eyeing the horse. Although Sergeant Slaughter and two others moved quickly, the black seemed to harbour no grudge against her rider. She had no killer's instinct and made no move towards the fallen youngster.

"Reckon we better look for another, young feller," said Slaughter. "Somehow this young mare don't seem to cotton to ya."

"Let me have another chance at her," pleaded Tim. "We'll get along all right once she gets to know me."

"She'll never git t' know ye, son, iffen ye don't stay with her longer," one of the troopers said.

This comment raised a laugh from the others that Tim chose to ignore. Once again he moved up alongside the black, who turned her head to look him over again.

"We'll see this time, old girl," said Tim as he vaulted into the saddle.

The mare started to buck again, fighting the bit. It took all Tim's strength to hold her head up, but hold it up he did.

"Open the gate," cried Tim.

One of the troopers swung the gate open and Tim let the mare run. He felt an exhilaration as the black tore down the trail. He let her run for about a half mile, then brought her to a trot, turned her, and swung her towards the barn again. He shifted his weight on the saddle, and as he did so the intelligent mare broke into a single-foot. Tim rode proudly into the barnyard and swung out of the saddle. He held the new mount's head and stroked her nose.

"She'll be all right now," he said to Slaughter. "She just didn't know me."

The sergeant looked at the black as she stood quietly. He scratched his head. "Maybe you're right at that, trooper." He looked her over with a critical eye. "She sure can run. Reckon a Yankee'll have his hands full catchin' you on her." He walked around her slowly. "She's black all right, black as midnight."

Tim looked at the mare. Midnight. The name seemed to fit her in all respects. "That's what I'll call her," he said.

"What's that?" asked Slaughter.

"Midnight," said Tim. "That's what I'll call her."

The older trooper glanced at her again. "Fits to a 'T'," he agreed.

CHAPTER SIX

REHEARSAL FOR THE REAL THING

IN THE following week, troopers moved in and out of the camp in both small and large groups. Tim, however, did not leave the immediate area. He found a trooper's life no easy one. Very quickly he learned that while the camp functioned with quiet efficiency, it did so only because each man had a share in camp routine. Tim cut wood, carried water for the cook, helped with the horses, and on two occasions stood picket duty with an older trooper. For the most part this work was done in addition to his trooper's training under Sergeant Slaughter's critical eye.

Although Hank Slaughter was not a very communicative person, Tim managed to piece together some of the man's background. He had served in the U.S. Cavalry for many years, first entering the service in the Mexican War. He had fought Indians, and was one of the best pistol shots in the South.

The sergeant usually took the boy to a small open meadow about a mile from the barn for training. The very first morning both troopers learned that Midnight had been trained to ignore gunfire. When Tim fired over or under her head at full gallop, her stride never faltered.

"That's the battle half won in trainin' a trooper's horse," said Slaughter admiringly. "Some horses just don't take to gunfire and never will."

"She even seems to like to smell gunsmoke," Tim agreed proudly.

Slaughter turned his attention to the young trooper. "Let's see how good you are." He walked to a nearby tree stump, placed a two-inch chip upright on its flat top, then moved out of range. "Let's see you hit that chip."

Tim drew his pistol, took careful aim and fired. The bullet creased the top of the stump six inches to the right of the chip.

He darted a quick look at the sergeant, aimed, and fired again. This time he missed by only two inches, again to the right. He cocked the pistol and, determined to hit the chip, took careful aim. As soon as he pulled the trigger, he knew he had hit the chip, and sure enough he saw it go spinning into the nearby brush. He looked at Slaughter expectantly.

"Middlin'," grunted the trooper. "But ain't no Yankee gonna give you all day to steady on him." He picked up another, smaller chip and put it in position. Backing off some fifteen paces, he spun, drew, and fired.

Tim saw the chip fly away. His mouth dropped open in amazement. Slaughter seemed to whirl, draw, and shoot in one blurred movement.

"Holy mackerel!" Tim said softly.

Slaughter grinned. "Takes a little practice, but you can do it too, son." He holstered his gun slowly, then added in a serious voice, "That's the kind of shootin' I want to see you do 'fore I let you out on a raid." He held up a hand as Tim started to protest. "Don't tell me you can't do it, because you have to. It's your best protection against a short life."

Tim soon realised that he was expected to exhibit similar accuracy, or almost so, while firing at a full gallop. He also learned to fire under Midnight's neck while hanging along her side. This position left only one foot exposed to enemy fire and gave the rider the maximum protection. Slaughter told him this was a trick that the U.S. Cavalry had picked up from the Plains Indians.

Tim also learned that he was expected to fire a rifle with equal dexterity. To his surprise, when Slaughter started rifle instruction, he gave the new trooper a brand-new Spencer repeating rifle. Tim had only heard of this fabulous weapon and knew that in the South these rifles were considered worth their weight in gold. Even in the North only a few regiments had been issued Spencers. When he commented on this, Slaughter shrugged.

"Mosby wants his Rangers to have the best Yankee money can buy," he answered dryly.

The session Tim disliked most was instruction in the use of the sabre. If anything, Slaughter was even more insistent that Tim use this weapon with greater ability than the rifle and the pistol. A trooper could always run out of ammunition or drop his firearm, but with the sabre knot tight around his wrist one could hold on to that gleaming blade under almost any circumstance short of actual unconsciousness.

The long, unfamiliar sabre felt heavy in Tim's hand, and as hour after hour of cutting, slashing, and parrying continued, he felt as if his arm would fall off of its own weight. But Slaughter kept the young trooper in training, pointing out his mistakes, showing him tricks with the weapon, until Tim came to realise that a sabre was perhaps a cavalryman's best friend.

One morning, after a week of this intensive drill, Tim was surprised to find Slaughter studying him critically as they rode towards the meadow. He flushed under the scrutiny and tried to ignore his instructor's appraisal.

"Reckon you got everything you need," said the older man, apparently satisfied. He looked off towards the Catoctin Mountains, in the west. "Report in this mornin' says the Yankees are gonna take a wagon train through Aldie Gap to-day. Captain wants us to look 'em over." He glanced at Tim again, and added, "Mind you, now, we'll probably see a parcel of blue-coats. Do everything I tell you *when* I tell you!"

"Yes, sir," said Tim eagerly.

He wondered whether Slaughter had told the Captain he could be trusted now as a fully-fledged trooper. Certainly the sergeant had said something to Mosby or he would not be going along on what amounted to a scout. Tim straightened up in his saddle and rode proudly alongside the older trooper. He sure wished Pa could see him now. Trooper Morgan!

Mosby had accurate information concerning the enemy's supply train, and a few hours later, as the two scouts rode on to the top of a small hill overlooking Little River Turnpike, Tim saw a long line of white-covered wagons crawling along the dusty road below. Up ahead, a full troop of blue cavalry rode in advance, and at the rear of the twenty wagons another full troop guarded the caravan.

"Lotsa protection," commented Slaughter. "Could be they wouldn't like to lose what's in them wagons."

He dug his heels into his horse's flanks. "Keep close to me. We'll go down and give 'em somethin' to think about."

Slaughter seemed to know the country well. As the two angled down the hillside, Tim could see that they were headed for a point to intersect the turnpike about a mile ahead of the train. He wondered whether the sergeant meant to ride down and actually look in the wagons, but since the order man spoke no more during the descent, Tim vowed to follow him right into the Yankee advance guard if that was where the sergeant was headed.

Near the foot of the hill, dense underbrush closed about them like a curtain, but Slaughter continued to follow a faint trail.

Suddenly the sergeant raised his hand and stopped. Tim pulled up Midnight and sat quietly while Slaughter peered through the underbrush. At length he turned to the boy.

"Here's the pike. We'll ride on to the road and let the Yankees in the advance troop see us. When they start chasin' us, we clear out fast." He looked at Tim sharply. "Don't get any ideas of your own. Follow right behind me."

Tim nodded. Why Slaughter wanted to show himself and then let the bluecoats chase them was beyond him, but Tim said nothing.

Slaughter moved forward, and, about fifty feet beyond, broke out of the brush on to the turnpike. He glanced over his shoulder to make sure Tim was following close behind.

"Mark that spot well. I aim to head back into the

woods right there. Won't be no time to look around for it neither."

Tim looked carefully at the faint opening in the brush, so he would be sure to remember the trail, then moved out after his companion.

In less than five minutes the two Rangers spotted the enemy troop on the road ahead. Tim saw one man wave, and the first squad spurred their horses into a run.

He glanced at Slaughter, who quietly sat his horse as though Yankees charged him every day.

Closer and closer drew the bluecoats, a cloud of dust rising behind the pounding hoofs of their mounts. Tim stole another glance at his sergeant. The bluecoats were getting mighty close, and the way they were charging down on them showed they meant business. Finally, when it seemed as if the Yankees could not miss, even with a pistol, the sergeant yelled, "Let's git!"

Slaughter let out a wild Rebel yell, whirled his horse, and pounded down the road away from the charging Yankees. Tim dug his heels in Midnight's flanks and felt her lunge forward after the sergeant's mount. Behind, he heard shrill yells and the sound of gunfire. He wondered how a whole squad could miss them.

"Here it is!"

Tim heard Slaughter's yell and watched him swing his horse off the road into the brush. Tim swung Midnight right behind the lead horse, protecting his eyes with his left arm as the black lunged through the growth. In minutes the two Rangers were in the clear again on the other side of the growth of brush. Slaughter drove his mount back up along the way they had descended until he reached a small stand of trees.

He rode in, threw himself from his horse, taking his Spencer with him. He dropped to one knee just as the first Yankee trooper emerged from the cover below. Slaughter opened up with his rifle and pumped several bullets down the hill.

Tim grabbed his Spencer and knelt beside the older Ranger. He saw the Yankee below fighting for control of his mount as he tried to back into the brush. Tim raised his rifle, but Slaughter motioned him not to fire.

"Let 'em stampede around in them briars for a while." he said calmly. "Then we trade a few more shots with 'em and skedaddle."

As Tim watched the underbrush below, he could hear Yankee troopers floundering around as they sought to control their frightened horses. After a few minutes, the wild noises in the underbrush subsided, and the bushes began to move in widely separated spots.

"They're on foot and scatterin' now," Slaughter said. "Let's let 'em know we're still here." He raised his gun and fired into the underbrush. Tim fired several shots at the brush himself, convinced he did not hit anything. As a matter of fact, he was not sure he wanted to hit anyone. He could not seem to get mad at the Yankees down there. They certainly had done nothing but chase him and fire a few wild shots at him. The whole affair seemed more like a game than a battle.

Any further thoughts were interrupted by scattered rifle fire from the troopers below. Tim heard the angry whine of Yankee bullets cutting through the growth of trees where he and Slaughter lay hidden. He raised himself slightly and looked over his shoulder to where Midnight stood calmly waiting, like the well-trained horse she was. He began to worry about her. If the Yankees should really start firing in earnest, she might get hit.

"Should I move the horses back farther?" he asked anxiously.

"Naw," answered the older man. "We'll scatter a few more shots in the brush and git out of here." He turned to look at the boy. "You ready to git after we let 'em have a few more rounds?"

Tim grinned. "Right behind you, Sergeant."

The two fired another dozen rounds into the brush, although no Yankee was in sight. Only an occasional movement of the underbrush indicated their presence.

"Now," said Slaughter quietly. He drew back from his position, both Rangers mounted quickly and headed up the hill. Tim could see that Slaughter was trying to keep behind the stand of trees to conceal their retreat. At length, when they reached the top of the hill, Slaughter pulled up his horse and studied the valley below. The wagon train was stopped, and about half of the rear-guard troop had moved forward to augment the advance troop. The remainder of the rear guard had spread out, their eyes scanning either side of the wagon train for a possible ambush.

"Reckon that oughta keep 'em busy for the rest of the day," said the sergeant, apparently satisfied with his day's work.

Tim put his rifle in the saddle holster and looked inquiringly at the veteran.

"I still don't see that we accomplished much, Sergeant."

"You'd be surprised," answered the other. "Them Yankees'll be chasin' and shootin' at spooks all the rest of the day. They'll think the woods is loaded with Rebels. Come night-time, they'll be dog tired. Tomorrow morning 'fore they get the sleep out of their eyes, Mosby'll take the train away from them."

Tim now began to see the strategy behind the little game that he and Slaughter had played. Had Mosby intended to attack the wagon train that day, he would never have sent two troopers to alert the Yankees. Yet after a day chasing will-o'-the-wisps, by nightfall the bluecoats would believe they had chased all Rebels away. Secure in that belief and tired after a day of beating the underbrush and forest, they would be no match for the real Ranger surprise attack at dawn.

"Now we'll go tell the Captain," said Slaughter. "He oughta be in camp up towards Aldie Gap by this time."

Tim looked up hopefully. "Are we going to join the Captain in the raid?" he asked.

"Could be. Mebbe Mosby'll let ye go and then again mebbe he won't."

Tim grinned as they rode along. He patted Midnight's neck. "I think we'll go along, old girl," he murmured confidently. At the sound of his voice, Midnight pricked up her ears.

CHAPTER SEVEN

RAID AT DAWN

BY LATE afternoon the two Rebel Rangers had reached the lower slopes of the Catoctin Mountains. They had sighted few people during the day, for Slaughter seemed to know all the back trails. During the early afternoon they had stopped at a friendly farmhouse. The old farmer and his wife fed them well on the limited supplies at hand.

Tim still blushed when he thought of how the old lady had clucked over him, repeating over and over how young he seemed for a soldier. He reckoned he was more of a soldier now than he had been when he got up that morning. Leastwise he'd been shot at. Funny thing about being shot at; he realised he hadn't been as scared as he thought he would. He could still see those Yankee troopers charging down the road at him, but he figured that Midnight could outrun any horse in Virginia, perhaps in the whole world. He stroked her neck again. The mare didn't seem to breathe heavily even after a full day's riding.

What other thoughts he might have had were interrupted by Slaughter pulling his horse to a halt. The older trooper listened carefully, then pursed his lips and gave an imitation of a bobwhite's call. After a slight pause he was answered by a similar, but muted, call from the forest ahead.

"They're here already," he said with satisfaction, and prodded his horse on.

Farther up the slope a grey-clad Ranger moved out from behind a tree and waved.

"See any Yankees, Hank?" he called to Slaughter.

The sergeant grinned. "Saw a few over on the pike chasin' rabbits," he answered. "Captain up at the camp?"

"Reckon so," replied the picket, "along with every other Ranger he could get together."

Tim leaned forward to hear all of the exchange. He had never seen more than two dozen Rangers together at one time. If Captain Mosby had called the whole of his command together, there was sure to be a raid. He was disappointed when Slaughter merely nodded and pressed on. Mosby's men never seemed to probe about what was going on.

The trail widened into a narrow glade between two hills, and Tim moved Midnight up alongside Slaughter.

"You suppose the Captain got all the Rangers together just for this raid?" he asked.

"Nope," answered Slaughter. "He could take them wagons with twenty men. Must be sumthin' else in the wind."

Up ahead, Tim could see a horse line with several men moving around the mounts. As the two came closer, they could make out troopers all over the glade busy at their many duties. The odour of horses and equipment mingled with the clean smell of the forest. Instinctively Tim realised that this sign might often be the first indication of a well-hidden camp. There was a certain orderliness about the place although the men did not seem to belong to any particular squad. Conspicuous by their absence were signs of tents or wagons or, in fact, any equipment that could not be carried on a trooper's mount. Even the men around the fires seemed to be using their own personal cooking gear. There was every sign that each man would be able to move out in a matter of minutes.

Tim let Midnight have her head as they drew closer. She followed the sergeant's mount to the horse line. Tim swung off her back and stripped the saddle.

"Rub 'em both down good," ordered Slaughter. "I'll report to the Captain."

Tim acknowledged the order and looked around for buckets to water the two mounts. He left the saddle blankets on both horses while he walked up and down the line in search of any available oats. Finding none, Tim promised himself he would never go off on a scout again without taking along some oats for Midnight. That was what she needed after a long day's ride.

Caring for the horses took the greater part of the next half hour, and Tim was so engrossed in his work that he did not hear Sergeant Slaughter until the man spoke behind him.

"Major wants to talk to you, son."

"Major?" asked Tim in surprise.

"Captain's been made a major. His commission just come in," Slaughter informed him. "Nobody keeps Mosby waitin'," he added meaningfully. "I'll finish the horses."

Tim made his way through the camp to the far end where several officers stood before the newly commissioned Major of Partisans. As usual, Mosby looked as if he had just finished dressing. His spotless grey uniform, topped by the scarlet-lined cavalry cloak, gave him an air of distinction above all others. Tim waited, several paces away from the group. He could see the long plume rising above the Major's pinned-up hat move as Mosby gave the officers their instructions. He saw the officers now salute and turn away. Now the commander glanced in Tim's direction, then motioned for him to approach.

Tim walked briskly up to his commander and saluted.

Mosby looked the boy over for a full minute before he spoke.

"You made a scout with Sergeant Slaughter this morning," he said rather than asked. "How did you like it?" Mosby kept his ice-blue eyes on the boy's face.

Tim thought for just a second. Mosby must know all about the scouting trip because he was sure that Slaughter had reported in detail. He wondered whether the Major was just making conversation.

"It was all right, sir," he began and, although realising he had made a rather weak statement, he didn't know what to add.

"Were you frightened at any time?"

Tim flushed. "Yes, sir. When those Yankees started charging us, I was scared until we started moving."

Mosby nodded grimly. "Good! Any man who won't admit to fear on occasion is either a fool or a liar." He paused a moment, never taking his eyes from Tim's face, then went on, "Do you think you're ready to go on a full-scale raid?"

Tim stood as straight as he could.

"Yes, sir!"

"Sergeant Slaughter tells me you're pretty good with your weapons," Mosby said.

"He sure has shown me a lot," acknowledged Tim modestly.

"And you've learned fast," added Mosby. "He also tells me you can obey orders. That's why I plan to let you go on a raid to-night."

"The wagon train?" asked Tim eagerly.

"The same," said Mosby. Of a sudden he became more formal. "You will ride with a group under Lieutenant Clayton. Don't take any chances and do exactly as you are told."

"Yes, sir!" replied Tim happily. He waited for Mosby to dismiss him, then hurried back to the horse line.

"The Captain—I mean Major, says I can go on the raid!" he informed the sergeant with unconcealed glee.

"Figgered he would," grunted Slaughter. "Now go get some firewood so we can get ourselves some supper." If Sergeant Slaughter shared his happiness at Tim's acceptance as a fully-fledged trooper, he did not show it.

Mosby's Partisan band moved out of the glade before sunrise at an easy trot. Though there was no talking in the ranks, Tim could almost feel the tension running through the horsemen. From snatches of conversation he had overheard the night before, the wagons must represent a valuable haul. But even more important was the rumour that Mosby meant to keep his whole command together after the raid, rather than scatter and wait for another call. There were also vague references to troop movements in the Shenandoah Valley, which could only mean that General Lee was finally moving his grey armies north towards Pennsylvania.

Tim quietly looked over the troopers nearest him and noticed that each rode with calm confidence. There seemed to be no regulation about a trooper's equipment or at least the amount he carried. Some rode with saddle-bags, others with only an oilskin bundle behind the saddle. Several men wore as many as six pistols, two in their belts, two in saddle holsters and two more tucked in the tops of their boots. Thirty-six shots in all! They were not likely to run out of ammunition in a quick raid! Without exception, on a raid each carried a sabre and a Spencer rifle. On this point, the Major insisted on uniformity.

Mosby, leading the troop with two lieutenants, quickened his pace when the horsemen broke on to the deserted turnpike. He held this speed for nearly five miles, then the pounding hoofs drumming on the hard road slowed suddenly to a walk. Tim saw two horsemen ride out of the timber bordering on the moonlit road ahead; their hands were held high. Mosby halted the troop and moved ahead with his two lieutenants. The men conferred, then Mosby motioned his Partisans forward. With a minimum of orders, the troop split into three groups at this point, one each heading into the timber on either side of the road and a third, under Mosby, proceeding down the road. Tim's group headed into the timber on his right, and he noticed Sergeant Slaughter's familiar figure in the same group. He had no idea why Mosby had split his force, no idea where he was headed, and he had received no instructions. He shrugged. When someone told him to do something, he reckoned he would, and that would be all there was to it. He did not see any other troopers receiving orders, so guessed they did not know any more than he.

Within the timber, Tim could barely make out the horse ahead of him. The soft carpet of pine needles muffled the sound of hoofs and only the squeak of leather and an occasional rattle of a sabre broke the stillness of early morning.

When the column did stop, Midnight almost overran the horse ahead. He heard a soft, "Dismount," ripple down the line and swung off his mare. Again the line walked forward and moved into a clearing. He eased up with the rest of the troopers until they were grouped around the lieutenant.

"Quiet," ordered the lieutenant, and in an instant the troopers had calmed their restless mounts.

"The only cover between us and the Yankee wagon camp," the officer said softly, "is about a hundred yards of timber. Beyond that is a meadow. From the timber to the camp is an open stretch of perhaps another hundred yards." The lieutenant paused and looked around the group for a moment while the men digested the situation. "On the other side of the camp another detail of our Rangers is hidden just as we are."

He paused again, then continued. "These are our instructions. The Major will initiate the attack and engage such of the guards as get to their mounts. Our other force will flank the Yankees after Mosby attacks. As soon as the engagement is general, this group will then cut out the wagons.

"By dawn the drivers will have the teams hitched up.

Mosby'll wait for that. Does everyone understand the plan of attack?" The lieutenant glanced around his command for questions.

Tim had questions, plenty of them, but he sure was not going to be the only one to speak up. The other troopers either kept silent or nodded their heads.

"Move quietly!" the lieutenant ordered softly. "Four men hold the horses. The rest follow me."

Tim, standing beside Midnight, suddenly found himself holding the reins of a half-dozen mounts as their riders handed them to him.

"So I'm a horse holder," he murmured to Midnight, as she shied away from the other horses in the group. He found he was not the only one, however. Three other troopers also held several mounts. Tim moved as close to the next trooper as the reins would let him.

"Does this mean we won't get in the fight?" he asked in a hoarse whisper.

The other trooper laughed silently. "Don't fret, sonny. You'll see plenty of action 'fore this mornin's over."

Midnight, nervous among the other horses, drew Tim back to her side to soothe her. She quieted and nuzzled his cheek.

Tim wondered whether the Rangers really would take the camp by surprise. As the minutes wore on and light streaked the eastern sky, he began to check his pistols, straighten his sabre belt and fidget with his gauntlets. Finally he stripped the hot leather gauntlets off his hands and folded them under his belt. He began to wonder when the other troopers, presumably watching the Yankee camp, would return. The bluecoats were certainly stirring around now; he could hear the shouts of the teamsters getting their horses hitched to the wagons.

Suddenly he heard a rustling noise from the covering woods and saw the Rangers returning for their horses. As if in response to their movement, he heard a faint rattle of gunfire beyond the camp.

"Yankee pickets along the turnpike have picked up Mosby," cried the lieutenant. "Mount and follow me!" The Ranger officer swung into his saddle and moved towards the woods.

Troopers quickly snatched their horses, and Tim vaulted into the saddle. He crowded up into the centre of the detail heading into the woods and found himself beside Sergeant Slaughter.

The veteran trooper eyed the boy sharply, then said, "Ride beside me. And watch yourself!"

Tim nodded and felt his stomach tighten. The men around him looked grim in the grey light. There were no smiles; an almost electric tension gripped them all.

Just before they reached the meadow, the detail halted again. Noise from the Yankee camp was now a confused roar. Through the remaining trees, Tim saw Mosby's grey-clad troopers charging in from the south. Yankee cavalry men scurried around the camp, cursing and screaming for their mounts. The dust cloud above Mosby's troop grew closer and closer. A Federal officer was vainly trying to rally his guard, but before the Yankees could gather for the defence, Mosby would be on them.

Barely half the wagon guard met Mosby's charge,

and the force of the Ranger's strike rolled the defenders back. On the other side of the wagon train another Yankee officer gathered the remainder of the guard and prepared to charge into the mêlée. In good formation they swept around the end of the wagons to flank Mosby's men.

At this moment, Tim caught a movement in the woods on the far side of the camp, as the other detail of Rangers swooped out of their hiding place. They came quartering down the slight slope, and the fresh half of the Yankee guard, intent on Mosby's action ahead, failed to see them in time. The Rangers moved in fast, cutting through the Yankees until the action became a confused mass of swinging sabres amidst rising clouds of dust kicked up by frenzied horses.

"Charge!"

The order caught Tim by surprise as he sat his horse watching open-mouthed the scene in the meadow. Midnight lunged with the other Ranger mounts, and Tim found himself racing across the meadow. All around him Rangers screamed their wild Rebel yell.

Lieutenant Clayton headed for the wagons as planned, ignoring the savage fighting. He pounded to the lead wagon with Sergeant Slaughter and Tim right behind. Midnight, excited by the noise, would have passed the officer had Tim not held her back.

"Grab the lead horses and get 'em moving!" shouted the Ranger officer over his shoulder.

Slaughter pulled his mount to a sliding halt alongside the first team and fought the lead horse for control. Tim pulled Midnight in alongside the second team and grabbed the reins of their leader. Out of the corner of his eye he saw the frightened civilian teamster hanging on to the reins as if frozen to the seat.

"Get this team moving!" he shouted and waved his pistol to emphasise his order.

The teamster, terror-stricken, could do nothing. Tim slapped the lead horse's flanks, yelling at the top of his lungs. The horse reared, then lunged forward wildly.

"Control your team!" he screamed above the roar of the battle.

The teamster still remained inert until Tim moved back beside the seat and levelled his pistol at a point midway between the two frightened eyes.

"Wake up or I'll blow you off that seat!" he yelled.

"Yes, sir! Yes, sir!" screamed the driver, and he began to fight to control his team.

Slaughter had his wagon moving smartly, but Tim could see virtually nothing to the rear because of the heavy dust. He wondered which way the lieutenant intended taking the wagons, but figured as long as he kept in line he would be all right. From what he could see the raid was a rousing success.

Suddenly he heard a warning shout ahead and saw the lieutenant wheel his horse to meet the attack of a blue-clad trooper roaring out of the dust to the right. He saw the Ranger officer whip out his sabre, saw the blade twist as the lieutenant took a cross stroke from the Yankee.

Slaughter left his team to aid the lieutenant, but was immediately engaged by a second Union cavalryman. A third Yankee came racing out of the dust, and Tim saw him angle towards Slaughter, who already had his hands full.

Tim dug his heels in Midnight's flank. The mare darted forward like a black streak. The young trooper pulled her to the left to intercept the rider bearing down on the sergeant. The mare never faltered. She sideswiped the Yankee with a jolting slam. The bluecoat left his saddle and went rolling on the ground. Tim pulled Midnight up short, wheeled and charged the Yankee sitting helplessly in the dust. The Yankee sat half dazed, sabre on the ground beside him. At full gallop Tim levelled his pistol at the cavalryman. . . . Then suddenly recognition dawned! The bluecoat on the ground was Murphy!

Tim lowered the weapon, grinned at the fallen trooper, and spurred Midnight ahead to catch his wagon.

The lieutenant's adversary was nowhere in sight; Slaughter's trooper lay still on the ground. In the distance Mosby's men were chasing the remainder of the blue cavalry down the turnpike.

Tim caught up with his wagon and noticed that his teamster was driving as if his life depended on it. Up ahead the lieutenant, now back in his place at the head of the train, kept urging the first driver to greater speed. The wagons spread out and by the time the leader rolled out of the meadow and back on to the turnpike, they were well strung out.

Slaughter rejoined the wagon ahead of Tim, and the lieutenant galloped back down the line, crying, "Close up," to each trooper and wagon.

After about fifteen minutes of this breakneck pace, when Tim had begun to wonder if the lieutenant intended to kill all the teams, he saw the wagon ahead slow down, then stop. Behind he could hear the "Whoas" of the other drivers.

"Send all teamsters back," the order came bellowing down the line.

Tim motioned his frightened driver down from the seat and said, "All right, friend, that's you. Get moving towards the rear."

When the drivers had been herded back along the road, Tim followed Slaughter's example and tethered Midnight to the tail gate. Then he climbed to the driver's seat and took up the reins.

Much to his surprise, the wagon train stopped again just around the next curve. While he was wondering what the next move might be, Mosby and his Rangers came alongside.

"Let's take a look, boys," shouted the Partisan Major. "We'll take what we want and burn the rest."

For the most part the wagons contained forage, subsistence stores, regimental and headquarters supplies, but one was loaded with new Spencer rifles.

Mosby was delighted. General Stuart had directed him to obtain all the new rifles he could. He ordered the wagons to move on to the next clearing where they were pulled off the turnpike. Rangers unhitched the teams and lead-tied them into strings for easy handling. The rifles were carried up a hillside and cached. Such other stores as could be carried on horseback were separated into packs, and the remainder grouped with the wagons for burning. Bluecoat reinforcements could be expected at any moment from both directions on the turnpike; therefore the wagons were quickly fired.

Tim studied Mosby as he sat watching flames climb up the wagon covers, and wondered whether he, too, was thinking what a terrible waste war was.

Finally the wiry commander raised his white gauntlet, gestured forward, and headed for the forested mountain in the distance.

As the victorious raiders moved along the trail, Slaughter rode up beside Tim until the two were stirrup to stirrup.

"You all right, Tim?" he asked.

"Yes, sir—I mean Sergeant," he answered. "I'm fine."

"Thanks for taking that Yankee off my back," said Slaughter warmly. "I hope I can do the same for you sometime." He looked at the boy questioningly. "How come you didn't finish that bluecoat off? You had him dead to rights."

Tim flushed. "I—well, it's a long story."

Slaughter grinned. "Tell me sometime."

"I will, Sergeant."

"Let's drop that sergeant, boy. Just call me Hank. Every other trooper does." He touched his spurs to his mount and moved on up the line.

Tim looked after the veteran gratefully. He felt pretty good about the raid. He had not made any mistakes and had downed a Yankee at that. Suddenly a thought struck him. He had not fired a single shot and his sabre had stayed in its scabbard, forgotten during the whole raid!

CHAPTER EIGHT

RETURN OF A BULLY

TIM THOUGHT that the Rangers would get a rest after the raid on the wagon train, but he was mistaken. Mosby headed directly for the Bull Run Mountains to the south of Aldie Gap. By nightfall the full troop followed their leader single file over the mountain along an unguarded bridle trail. The line moved on and on, and it was nearly dawn before the Partisan leader gave the order to dismount in the front yard of a large farmhouse. Tim followed the other troopers and, after taking care of his mount, spread an oilskin on the ground and dropped into an exhausted sleep.

He had been asleep no more than an hour, it seemed, when the several sergeants of the command walked among the sleeping men and prodded them awake.

"Rise and shine, troopers," the word went around. "Big doin's to-day!"

Tim wondered vaguely what the "big doin's" might be, but when he saw several Rangers emerging from the house with great pans of steaming food, all thought of raids or war left his mind. He was ravenous.

As he stood there eyeing the food, Hank Slaughter moved up behind him, grabbed his arm and propelled him to the centre of the lawn where troopers were fast gathering.

"Move, boy. Let's try to fill up those hollow legs," Hank said.

That was all the prodding the boy needed. He took a heaped plate from one of the cook detail and ate steadily until the food was gone. In no time at all one of the cooks passing among the troopers refilled the boy's plate, and this was soon scraped clean again. Tim heaved a sigh of satisfaction, and put the plate beside him on the grass.

"You ain't stoppin' yet, are you boy?" called one trooper. "You better eat like you don't know when you'll get your next meal."

"Which he don't," added another, amid raucous laughter from the rest of the group.

Tim took the ribbing good-naturedly. These Partisans of Mosby, who were hated and called bandits by the North, were the most amazing group of men he had ever seen. They could be deadly killers one minute and skylark like boys the next. But one characteristic stood out above all others; they were always alert for danger, ready to ride or fight in an instant.

The informality of the after-breakfast banter was quickly halted when Mosby himself appeared. He paused for a moment on the top step of the house, drew on his long white gauntlets and surveyed the lawn. Older members of the troop hurried to their mounts. Mosby was ready to ride, and he was not a man to brook delay.

"Saddle up!" bellowed the sergeants.

Soon the calm of morning was broken by the noise of troopers getting their mounts ready.

Tim had Midnight's saddle on and was cinching the girth when a trooper led Mosby's big grey up to he steps. The Partisan leader mounted, raised his hand and galloped out of the yard. His troopers thundered after him, few knowing where they were going.

They soon found out. At Rector's Cross Roads, a few miles from the farmhouse, Mosby led his men into a large clearing. At least fifty grey-clad troopers waited in the clearing, and others were riding in. When they were all assembled, Tim figured there were at least a hundred.

Mosby stood in his stirrups and raised his voice. "Men! On orders from the Confederate War Department, we are organising the Rangers into the 43rd Battalion of Partisan Rangers." His gaze seemed to include each individual Ranger. "Anyone who does not wish to join this battalion is under no compulsion to do so. He may leave now. Those wishing to remain will give their names to the sergeant."

He nodded towards a sergeant sitting on a log, a pad of official-looking paper in his hand. Beside this trooper sat a civilian who, Tim later learned, was a representative from the War Department.

Tim joined the long line of men filing by the sergeant and gave his name. On stating his age, he saw the civilian glance at him sharply. Tim did not worry; he knew Major Mosby would back up his enrolment, even though he was but sixteen.

A short time later Mosby mounted his horse and bade the men line up in the clearing.

"We are now going to vote on your officers as required by the Articles of War. These are the men you will vote for."

Slowly and clearly the major read out the list of officers, a captain, and three lieutenants.

"All in favour of these men?" The Partisan chief looked up and down the line.

A thundering chorus of "Ayes" swept over the new battalion.

"Then they are so appointed," said Mosby clearly. He walked his horse to the civilian. "You can tell the Secretary of War that in accordance with the Articles of War we have held an election of officers and the 43rd Battalion is formed."

The civilian grinned. "I'll do that, sir. Shortest election I've ever witnessed."

The new 43rd Battalion left the clearing in company formation. Tim found himself in a detail with Slaughter as platoon sergeant. He considered himself lucky to be in the first platoon where he not only liked the sergeant, but Mosby also rode at point with Captain Foster, the newly elected Company Commander. It felt good to be in a regular army cavalry unit, even if the 43rd would act independently of the rest of the army.

Major Mosby seasoned the company with a hard ride north to the Potomac, where the command forded the river at Seneca Ford and attacked a unit of the Federal Sixth Michigan Cavalry. The Yankees, caught as usual by surprise, put up a stiff fight, but were driven off. Tim helped burn a canal-boat on the Chesapeake and Ohio Canal, as the Rangers destroyed all Federal stores they could find. Then he was back in the saddle again, fording the Potomac as the battalion headed south once more.

The next day Mosby led his men into General Stuart's headquarters camp at Middleburg, west of Bull Run Mountains. They rode in, dead tired from two days in the saddle. Tim looked forward to a soft spot on the ground where he could curl up and sleep.

"Morgan!" Sergeant Slaughter's sharp call brought Tim to attention.

"Yes, sir."

"We ride with the Major to headquarters tent."

"Yes, sir!"

Tim dug his heels into Midnight and took up position behind the Partisan chief.

Mosby seemed to know where he was going as he threaded the big grey through the vast Confederate camp. It was Tim's first glimpse of the regular army, and he was amazed at the number of soldiers assembled in one place. He knew that General Stuart had been promoted and had five full brigades under his command but he had never realised what this meant until confronted by row after row of tents and the several artillery parks. The whole valley around the little town of Middleburg seemed alive with grey-clad soldiers. He forgot his weariness at the sight of so much army, and before he realised it, Mosby had dismounted in front of a large tent.

"Hold the horses," ordered Slaughter. He swung off his horse and moved to a position a few paces behind the Major.

Tim jumped off his horse, grabbed the reins of the other two, and stood quietly watching the tent. In a moment a stocky, squarely built man in the uniform of a general swept aside the tent flaps and strode over to the Partisan chief. General Stuart's big bushy brown beard hid the collars of his uniform, but Tim could see the rest of the elaborately braided jacket with its red sabre sash. Over his shoulder Stuart had thrown a cape with a corner turned back to reveal a bright red lining. A great long plume stood out from his cavalryman's wide-brimmed hat. Tim could see why most men and certainly all the ladies of the Confederacy called the General "dashing."

The two officers talked earnestly for about five minutes, then, as Mosby took his leave, the General put his arm around Mosby's shoulder and walked with him to where Tim held the horses.

General Stuart, a known admirer of good horseflesh, ran a critical eye over Tim's black mare. He left the Major and walked around Midnight, noting all her good points.

"Which one of your men rides this fine animal, John?"

"Trooper Morgan, sir," answered Mosby. "If the black pleases you, I'm sure Morgan won't object to letting you have her."

Tim's heart sank. Slaughter took the reins of the other two mounts from the boy's hand and moved them away so that the General could get a good look at Midnight.

"Your horse?" General Stuart paused, looked the boy over, and said, "How old are you, son?"

Tim stood as straight as he could, "Sixteen, sir."

"My God, John! How young do you take 'em in the 43rd?"

Tim could feel his cheeks redden.

"I'll match young Morgan against most of your cavalrymen, sir," said Mosby.

"I'll take your word for it. He certainly knows how

to pick horses." Stuart turned again to the black. "Hold your head up, young lady," he said to Midnight and reached out to stroke her nose.

Midnight threw back her head, rolled her eyes white, then snapped viciously at the outstretched hand.

As the General stepped back, Tim grabbed Midnight by the bridle. He murmured gently to calm her down.

"I'm sorry, General," he said, voice quaking. "She's a mite touchy with strangers."

The General surveyed the boy and horse shrewdly before he said, "One-man horse, eh, son?"

Tim swallowed hard and darted a glance at Major Mosby. "I guess so, sir." He stroked Midnight's head affectionately.

"Well, son, don't worry," said Stuart. "She's too small for my taste. You keep your horse." He paused, lowered his eyebrows and stared sternly at Tim. "And take care of her. She's a fine mare."

"You bet I will, General," answered Tim. "Midnight and I get along fine."

"I'm sure you do."

General Stuart, dismissing further talk on the matter, turned again to the Partisan chieftain. "Find out all you can of the Yankee strength, John. And remember we need horses and mules—lots of 'em! Bring me Yankee prisoners, and bring 'em in good health. I need information."

"You'll get them, General," answered Mosby confidently. He saluted and swung into the saddle. Sergeant Slaughter and Tim mounted and, as Mosby walked his horse back through the camp, they fell in behind.

Tim soon found that the 43rd Battalion had discovered a place to rest in a grove of trees south of the main camp. He fed and watered Midnight and the Major's grey after the officer dismissed him, then gratefully sank to the ground for a much needed rest.

But the 43rd had its orders, and weary as he might be, by midnight Tim was again in the saddle with the rest of the battalion. This time he could guess where they were headed—back across the Bull Run Mountains into Federal-controlled country for those horses and mules which General Stuart requested.

Mosby spared neither horses nor men to secure the equipment and livestock the Confederate Army needed. One night he would hit a wagon train with the full company of the 43rd; the next, he would divide the men into three or four groups and hit widely separated Federal outposts. The Union commanders detailed companies, then battalions, and finally a regiment to track down the elusive raider. They failed because Mosby hit with the speed of an arrow.

While the Rangers had been left pretty much to their own devices in the choice of uniforms, the 43rd gradually attained standard dress. This consisted of grey pantaloons with a yellow cord down the seams, dark jackets, and grey felt hats, one side turned up and fastened with a rosette, a black feather sticking up on the other side.

It was after one of their lightning raids, when the Rangers had returned to a temporary camp, that a dusty trooper walked over to Tim as he sat eating his cold supper.

"You Morgan?" The hard-eyed cavalryman looked him over carefully.

Tim stood up. "Why, yes," he answered.

"I saw your pa last night. He told me to tell you he's fine." The man kept looking at him curiously. "Reckon he must be real proud of you. Told me he'd been hearin' about you from time to time." The man paused. "From the way he talked I'd expected an older boy."

Tim bristled. Though delighted to hear from Pa, he was getting mighty tired of everyone commenting on his age.

"I don't want to seem ungrateful for the information, but I reckon I'm old enough."

The trooper stared coldly at him. "Don't get feisty. I guess you are, at that." He turned and started to leave, then swung around to face the boy again. "By the way, he said to tell you Nellie's fine, too. She your girl?"

Tim darted a look at the horse line where Midnight stood, her head up, watching him. "I guess you might say she's one of 'em," he replied with a grin.

The man gave Tim a sarcastic look and turned away again with a "Hmmph."

Hank Slaughter came over to Tim and nodded towards the departing trooper.

"What'd he want, Tim?" he demanded.

"He saw Pa last night. Says he's all right."

"Good," grunted the sergeant. "Now suppose you and me get saddled up."

"Another raid?" asked Tim wearily.

"Just you and me this time," replied Slaughter. "A little scout." He walked towards the horse line. "We'll get our orders from the Major."

Soon the two troopers stood before the Partisan chieftain who was seated as usual at his small field desk. His ice-blue eyes sweeping over their equipment seemed to confirm that they were prepared in every respect.

"I need some information about Yankee troop movements between here and the Potomac," he began. "You will scout a line east of the Catoctin Mountains north to Seneca Ford." Mosby let that thought sink in for a moment, then continued, "General Hancock's Union Corps has been quiet too long. He's due to move, and I want to know which way he moves."

The Major moved an oil lamp closer to the paper on his desk. "Look at this map." He pointed to Aldie Gap. "General Pleasanton, with the Yankee cavalry, is scattered around Aldie. He's trying to find out what Stuart is up to. The Yankees have plenty of pickets out and scouts all over the country. Don't take any chances; avoid them!"

"Yes, sir," answered Slaughter. "We will."

"Your primary job is to scout Seneca Ford. Learn where the enemy pickets are. Learn camp dispositions. When Stuart arrives at the ford with his brigades, we must give him accurate information."

"I understand, sir," answered Slaughter again. "How do we get the information to General Stuart?"

"I will arrive with the battalion at the old Davis farm five miles south of the ford at noon two days from now. Meet me there. I'll get your information to Stuart." He considered the two troopers. "Do you understand all my instructions?"

"Yes, sir, Major. We'll have all the information when you get there."

Mosby turned his eyes on Tim. "Do you understand, Morgan? If anything happened to the sergeant, could you carry on?"

"Yes, sir," answered Tim firmly. "And I know where the Davis farm is."

"Good!" said Mosby satisfied. "You may go now. And be careful. I want information, not heroics!"

The two troopers saluted and swung into the saddle. As they rode out of the camp, they saw two strange horsemen, followed by a trooper of the 43rd, entering the camp. Tim, conscious only of the responsibility Mosby had placed on them, gave the two strangers only a passing glance. He noted briefly that both seemed much the worse for wear, and were dressed in ragged civilian clothing, with slouch hats drawn down over their eyes.

About a mile out of camp, Tim began to think about the two strangers. Something about the larger man seemed familiar. A vague uneasiness troubled him. Suddenly he let out a shout.

"Hank! Those strangers back there!"

Slaughter jerked his mount to a halt and drew his Colt in one motion. "Where?" He darted a quick glance around the countryside.

"No, no! I mean those two we saw riding into camp as we left," Tim said excitedly. "One of them was Bull Ruffing!"

"So what," said Slaughter disgustedly. "Who the devil is Bull Ruffing?"

"You remember, Hank. The Yankee trooper I told

you about. The deserter that shot Pa." Tim swung Midnight around. "Let's go back and tell the Major!"

"Steady now," cautioned the older trooper. "The Major gave us a job to do."

"But, Hank," pleaded Tim. "There's no telling what that man's up to. We ought to warn the Major."

Slaughter pondered the matter for a moment, then agreed reluctantly. "We'll take the time to go back," he grumbled, "but probably we'll have to ride all night to make up for lost time."

Tim kept Midnight at a fast pace all the way back to camp. Only when they reached the camp's vedettes, did Slaughter order him to slow down.

"You go ridin' into camp at this speed and either the pickets'll shoot you or you'll have the whole camp up in arms," he warned.

Tim, although impatient to get to the Major, saw the wisdom of this and slowed Midnight to a fast walk.

Mosby looked up sharply when Tim pulled his horse to a stop in front of his desk.

Tim jumped off his horse, hastily saluted and blurted out breathlessly, "Sir, those two strangers that rode into camp. Where are they?"

"Trooper Morgan," Mosby said in a level tone. "Let me remind you that it is customary to get an officer's permission to speak first. Let me also remind you that you are presumably under orders to perform scout duty." He turned his cold eyes on Slaughter. "Explain the meaning of this, Sergeant."

"With the Major's permission, sir, I think you'd better hear the lad's story," Slaughter replied.

Mosby turned to Tim. "All right. Let's hear it."

Tim flushed under the Partisan chief's scrutiny. "I'm sorry, sir. I guess I was excited," he apologised, "but one of those strangers who rode into camp a while back was Bull Ruffing, the Yankee deserter who shot Pa."

Mosby's manner changed completely. "Are you sure?" he asked sharply.

"Yes, sir," replied Tim emphatically. "I'd stake my life on it!"

"Corporal of the guard!" shouted Mosby.

A trooper, fully armed, came running to the Major.

"Those men who rode into camp about half an hour ago, where did they go?"

"Why—why, sir, when you told 'em they couldn't join up, they left," said the flustered corporal of the guard. "You didn't say to hold them," he added defensively.

"Which way did they go?" Mosby snapped.

"To the west, sir," answered the guard, "towards the mountains."

Mosby thought for a minute. "It would take a score of men to find them up in the mountains to-night," he mused half aloud, then looked at Tim. "Thanks for the warning. Fortunately I didn't like their looks and refused to sign them up. I doubt whether they can do any mischief, but I'll send a detail out in the morning for a quick look. Now you two get on with your scout."

"Yes, sir," replied Slaughter. "Tim and me'll make up for lost time. Mount up, Tim," he ordered. "We got work to do."

CHAPTER NINE

GET THE WORD TO MOSBY

TIM LAY behind a screen of willows on a bluff overlooking the ford above Seneca Falls on the Potomac. He could see the bluecoats across the river on the Maryland side. He had been watching them since daybreak and they did not act as if there was a Johnny-Reb within a hundred miles. They went about their camp routine as calmly as if they were far removed from war. Tim felt a sense of satisfaction at this situation because it meant troops north of the river had not as yet been alerted to any Confederate move to the north. He was surprised but happy to find no Yankee pickets on his side of the river. That gave him and Hank a chance to look around. Thinking of Hank, he raised his head to peer up and down the river-bank. He wished the sergeant would return. Almost involuntarily he wiped the sweat off his forehead and realised the day was going to be a scorcher. With eyes wandering to the placid river below, he wished he could shed his clothes and take a swim. Never had water looked so inviting.

Although Tim had expected the sergeant to return soon from his hiding place upriver, he was startled by a low whistle behind him. He drew his pistol as a precaution and answered with a similar whistle. Moments later, Slaughter slithered through the brush and lay panting beside the boy. He glanced at the pistol and then at Tim.

"Ain't takin' any chances, eh?" he said with a grin.

Tim shook his head. "Not with all these bluecoats around." He holstered his gun. "From what I can see, looks like a regiment across the river."

Hank nodded. "At least a lot more'n when we hit 'em last time." He scanned the opposite river-bank. "See any canal-boats?"

The Chesapeake and Ohio Canal paralleled the river on the Maryland side, and the Federals had been moving material by canal-boat to augment their wagon transport.

"I've counted fifteen since daybreak," answered Tim.

"Any troops on 'em?" asked Slaughter.

"Only guards," replied Tim, "and most of them looked like they were asleep."

"Good. Let 'em sleep. We'll have to cross that canal after dark."

"We're going to cross the river?"

"Come dark," answered the sergeant. "We'll move on down the river, cross over, and make a swing around the Yankee camp. We gotta find out if there's any artillery coverin' the ford."

"What about the horses?" Tim asked. He wondered how Midnight was making out. They had tethered the animals in a deep ravine about a mile south of the river and they had made their way from there on foot. Tim could not help worrying that some straggler might discover the hiding place.

"Chance we'll have to take," Hank said. "We go stampin' 'round the Yankee camp on horses and they'll find us sure." He took a long look at the encampment. "As it is, unless the Yankees are sound sleepers, we'll have to walk mighty soft." Slaughter glanced sharply at the boy. "You catch some sleep now," he said. "I'll keep a lookout and wake you in about four hours."

At once Tim dropped off to sleep in spite of the hot, sultry weather. By mid-afternoon, he awoke to find the sergeant still alert.

"Feel better?" he asked, as Tim rubbed the sleep from his eyes.

"Why didn't you wake me?" the boy demanded, a bit irritated. He knew that Slaughter was as tired as he was.

"We can't move anyway 'fore dark," Hank replied calmly. "Plenty of time." He showed Tim a sketch of the river and the area surrounding the ford. "I've marked down supply areas, horse lines, tents, and anything else I could see. You look it over and add whatever I've missed." He lay back wearily on the ground. "Call if you need me," he mumbled and was instantly asleep.

Tim studied the crude map carefully. Slaughter had drawn in about everything, leaving little for him to add. Tim did take time to smooth out the lines and make the drawing more presentable. Time moved uneventfully on, then suddenly Tim saw a movement on a rise behind the camp. By pure luck, he sighted a fieldpiece being hauled into position by Federal artillerymen. When, earlier, he had heard the sound of axes, he had thought that only a wood-gathering detail was at work. Now, catching a glimpse of the gun through the trees, Tim realised that the fallen striplings were being used to conceal the gun's position. He marked the exact spot on his map. How lucky he was to have spotted it!

If there was one gun in place, there were probably more. . . . He spent the remainder of the afternoon scanning the far side of the river for possible gun positions. He discovered what might be three more, all carefully concealed. These he placed on the map with small question marks alongside them.

When Slaughter awoke, he showed him the map and pointed out the camouflaged gun.

The sergeant studied the paper carefully, then searched the woods behind the Yankee camp.

"I think you're right, Tim," he said. "Good thing you caught sight of that first gun. They've done a good job of keeping their artillery hidden." He glanced at the ford below them. "Reckon they've got the ford ranged, too. If Stuart tries to cross here without puttin' those guns out, he'll lose a lot of men."

"How will the General manage?" Tim asked. "Looks to me like he'll have to cross to get at them."

"Maybe," answered the other. "By the time Stuart got artillery in place on this side, those Yankee guns would have 'em cut down." He took another long look at the Yankee camp. "Reckon Mosby'd better silence those guns 'fore Stuart gets here. If there are any more, we better find out about them." He moved back from the bluff's edge and stood up. "Let's head down-river and see if we can find a place to cross."

By nightfall they had found exactly what they were looking for. Drawn up along the river-bank was an old skiff usable for the crossing. One nearby house seemed totally abandoned. Tim and Hank waited until after dark, then poled the boat quietly to the other side of the river. After drawing the small craft up under the willows, they climbed the bank to take a look at the canal. Looking up and down the straight stretch of water, they could see no boat traffic.

"Looks like we get wet," said Slaughter softly. "Won't be any bridges across down this way and even if there was, there'd be a Yankee guard on 'em." He removed the two pistols from his belt and took off his jacket and boots. "You swim?" he asked Tim.

Tim said he could and removed his boots.

"Drop your pistol in your boot and swim with one hand if you can," cautioned the sergeant. "Don't make any noise if you can help it. It ain't mor'n a good jump across this canal, anyway."

Tim found the water colder than he had expected, and, being forced to swim with one hand only, he was mighty glad that the canal was narrow. He heard Slaughter breathing heavily as they crawled up the bank on the far side.

"Whew!" the sergeant gasped, "glad we didn't have to swim the river, too." He stood up and listened intently. After a moment he sat down and started to haul his boots on. "Get your boots on, Tim; we got a long walk."

Tim looked around the deep woods confronting them. "How are we going to find any guns in the dark?" he asked.

"There are plenty of open fields around the ford," Hank replied. "We know about where the guns are, anyway. We'll work our way north of the river and double back towards the camp. When we get near the batteries, I suspect we'll see a camp-fire close to each. A gun's crew usually beds down near their gun."

They worked their way through a narrow fringe of timber screening the canal and found themselves in an orchard. Then, moving quietly through the trees, they came to an open meadow. The sergeant studied the field carefully, then pushed boldly out of the orchard.

"Keep hunched down and follow me," he said. "There might be a road on the other side of the meadow. If you hear or see anything, flatten out on the ground and don't move 'til you see me move."

The two worked their way across the field, and there in the open Tim felt there must be a thousand Yankee eyes on them. But soon they reached a road without incident.

"This road must lead to the ford," said Tim.

"Reckon so. Let's head back along it."

Hank struck out towards the south again.

Suddenly Tim saw Slaughter raise a hand, stop, then lean down and place an ear on the hard-packed road. He stood up quickly.

"Horses comin'!" he warned. "Let's get off the road."

Swiftly they jumped a ditch bordering the road and ducked behind a split-rail fence. Soon a troop of horsemen came pounding by, headed for the camp at the river. Tim could hear the squeak of leather and the clanking of sabres as clearly as if he had been one of the riders.

When they had passed, he whispered, "You figure they were looking for anything in particular?"

"Nah," answered Slaughter. "Just a patrol gettin' back late." He stood up and stared into the darkness. "Let's go find those guns."

They located the first battery without difficulty. As Hank had predicted, the soldiers had a camp-fire near the gun. The two Confederates crawled up close and, peering through the screen of underbrush, looked the battery over. The gun was in place, and as Tim had pointed out, it was partially concealed behind freshly cut timber.

Tim crawled back quietly when Slaughter touched him on the shoulder. When they were clear of the battery, Hank stopped.

"The other batteries will probably be set up on this same ridge." He pointed to the vague outline of a low hill roughly paralleling the river but well back from it. "Come on, we'll follow the rise."

It took at least three hours for them to locate the other three batteries. Satisfied that there were no more, Slaughter then cleared the area, heading north, then east to get back to their skiff. When at last they returned to the familiar orchard, the sergeant sat down wearily under a tree. Tim dropped to the ground beside him.

"I been thinkin', Tim," Hank began. "We got ourselves a real chunk of information. One of us got to get it back to Mosby. If we run into trouble, we move in opposite directions. We don't wait for each other, but head straight for the Davis farm and wait for the Major. You understand?"

"I understand," said Tim quietly.

The information they had gathered that night was

full and clear. Tim recognised the importance to Mosby and Stuart of the hidden batteries.

Hank scrambled to his feet. "All right, let's go," he said.

Slaughter set a faster pace back to the woods bordering the canal. As they started through the timber, Tim tried his best to move as quietly as possible. The sergeant seemed to be able to see in the dark and moved as silently as an Indian. . . . But within a few yards of the footpath he tripped on a vine and fell heavily. The noise of his fall seemed to shatter the quiet of the night.

Tim moved up quickly to his side. "You hurt, Hank?" he asked anxiously.

"Twisted my ankle a bit," muttered the sergeant. "It'll be all right."

Just then they heard the sound of running feet, and a voice called out from the path ahead, "Halt! Who goes there?"

Through the thin screen, Tim could see a soldier with a bull's-eye lantern standing on the path, peering into the woods.

"He'll have a swarm of bluecoats here in a minute," whispered Hank hoarsely. "I'm going to take him. When I do, you move fast and get across that canal. Head for the boat. Don't wait for me. If I don't follow right after you, get across the river in a hurry!"

"Who's in there?"

Tim could hear a tremor in the sentry's voice as he held the lantern up and tried to see into the timber.

The boy sensed Slaughter preparing for a lunge, and he too got ready to move. He heard the sergeant grunt, saw him dive out of the brush directly into the lamp.

"Corporal of the . . .!" The sentry's scream stopped abruptly as Hank's body catapulted into the surprised soldier.

Tim drove through the underbrush. He could see Hank on top of the desperately struggling sentry. Down the path he saw dancing lights and heard shouting.

"Get goin', Tim!" gasped Slaughter.

Tim waited no longer. He knew that Hank could take care of himself, and the sergeant's orders were explicit. He made a running dive into the canal, the momentum carrying him almost to the other side. As he scrambled up the bank, he darted a quick look down the path. The lights were dangerously close. He clawed his way to the footpath, rolled across it, and over the bank on the other side. Cautiously he stuck his head up. Why didn't Hank dive into the canal? Then he heard more scuffling directly across from him and realised that the Yankee sentry was putting up a desperate fight. Silently he blamed himself. Orders or no, he should have helped Hank. Maybe his ankle was worse than he had admitted. And then he saw it was too late. The first of the Yankee reinforcements gave a triumphant yell:

"We got him!"

Tim's heart sank. He could not help Hank now. He sat back numbly, eyes filling with tears of rage.

"One got away across the canal!" he heard the sentry shout.

Spurred into action by the words, Tim turned and plunged down the bank to the river. He shoved the skiff into the water, jumped in, and began to pole with all his strength.

By the time Tim had reached the Virginia bank, he could see lights moving along the opposite side of the river. The Yankees had lost no time sending out a search party to cover the Maryland bank. He paused only long enough for a quick look, then scrambled up the slope and plunged into the woods. Now that Hank was a prisoner, it was up to him to get the word to Mosby.

CHAPTER TEN

THIS WAS IT!

JOHN SINGLETON MOSBY sat quietly on the porch of the Davis home and listened to Tim's description of the Yankee camp and the battery emplacements. Without comment, he watched the boy's face as he told of Hank's capture, and the Major's eyes were briefly sympathetic. When Tim had finished, Mosby stood up and placed a fatherly hand on the young trooper's shoulder.

"You've learned to carry out orders, Tim," he said. "I know how you must have wanted to help Slaughter, but you did exactly as he wanted you to. Your information may save many lives." He paused for a moment and again became the Partisan chieftain. "Let's get in the house. I want you to draw a map like the one on Slaughter when he was captured. Can you do it?"

"Yes, sir," replied Tim. "I'm sure I can remember everything."

"Good," replied the Major.

They entered the house and he handed Tim paper and pencil. Tim carefully redrew the map as Major Mosby stood watching over his shoulder. When he had finished, the Partisan chief pointed to the battery farthest east.

"How far is it from the bank on the Virginia side to that battery?" he asked.

Tim frowned as he tried to think back. Slaughter had estimated the range from the ford to the battery at 1,500 yards; add another 100 yards for the distance to the bank, he thought. "About 1,600 yards, sir," he replied.

"How did you arrive at that figure?" demanded Mosby.

Tim told him.

"Fine," said the Major. "Now tell me, how many troops are encamped at the ford?"

"We figured about a regiment, Major," answered Tim, and then added, "not countin' the four batteries behind the camp."

"Did you see any infantry?"

"Not that we could tell, sir. It was a cavalry regiment." He went on to explain about the patrol they had seen during the night.

"Show me where you crossed the river," ordered Mosby.

Tim pointed to the approximate location of the skiff. "Right here, sir."

"You say you poled the skiff across?"

Tim nodded.

"How long was the pole?"

The young Ranger looked at his chief, puzzled by the question. "Well, sir——" He hesitated. "I guess it was about two feet taller than me."

"Don't guess," snapped Mosby. "Was it two feet taller than you?"

Tim thought back to the time he had cut the pole. "Yes, sir, two feet," he answered confidently.

"While you were poling the boat across, was there any spot where the pole wouldn't reach bottom?"

Tim looked up eagerly. Now he could see what the Major was driving at.

"No, sir. All the way across the river was not more than four or five feet deep, except the middle when I had to lean down to reach bottom." He thought back carefully. "I don't think that deeper part was more than twenty or twenty-five feet across and maybe six feet deep."

Mosby carefully studied the map, then gave a satisfied grunt. "I think we have all the information we need for the moment," he said at length.

Tim was conscious of the Major's eyes on him as he stood at attention,waiting to be dismissed.

"Eat and get some sleep," Mosby said. "We move out after dark and you show us the way."

He turned then and walked from the room.

Tim felt surging waves of weariness and suddenly realised that he had been on the move for almost twenty-four hours without sleep. His shoulders drooped as he walked out of the house and headed for the nearest cook fire.

Tim never realised how quietly a hundred men could move until he watched the 43rd Battalion proceed along the bank of the Potomac River east of Seneca Ford. Mosby had sent a small detail across the river after dark to silence any sentries along the canal. When three flashes of light signalled from the northern side of the river, the command to cross rippled softly down the line of horsemen. Fortunately, the light drizzle that had been falling all day had now turned into a steady rain and this provided excellent cover for the movement.

Tim found himself wondering whether he could remember the exact location of each battery. Major Mosby had explained the necessity of silencing those Federal guns. General Stuart, with three of his five brigades, intended to cross at Seneca Ford at dawn, but this was only part of the larger picture. Generals Lee, Longstreet, and A. P. Hill, with their armies, were moving north up the Shenandoah Valley. Federal forces were now alerted to the possible movement of Confederates into Maryland and Pennsylvania, and the Union generals were also on the move north. Stuart must get his cavalry across the Potomac quickly or he would run into Union General Hancock's Corps, also headed for Seneca Ford.

Tim, riding beside Mosby at the head of the column, wished mightily that Slaughter were there to help him with directions.

Midnight plunged into the river as if she wanted a swim.

"Keep beside me, Morgan! Can't you control that mare?" Mosby growled, as Midnight forged ahead of the big grey.

Tim fought the reins and pulled the mare back until the Partisan chief caught up. "Yes, sir," he said apologetically and kept abreast of his chief.

As the command moved across the river, Tim really began to worry. The steady rain blotted out all the familiar landmarks he had memorised. It was only when they reached the Maryland side that he recognised the spot where he had left the skiff. He saw a shadowy figure waiting on the bank.

"All clear along the canal?" Mosby asked impatiently.

"All clear, sir," answered the waiting Ranger softly. "Looks like we'll have to swim the mounts across the canal, though."

Mosby drew his oilskins closer around him. As he moved his head forward, water poured off the brim of his hat. "Doubt if we could get any wetter anyway," he growled. He rode up the bank to the canal towpath, then halted his mount and studied the situation. "Where do we go when we get across?" he asked Tim, without turning his head.

"Those trees cover only about fifty feet on the other side," explained Tim. "Past them, we'll be in an orchard."

"Any houses?" Mosby asked abruptly.

"No, sir. We didn't see any."

"All right, let's get moving," said the Major, and plunged his grey into the canal.

"Take the lead," he ordered Tim when they had crossed. He turned to a sergeant close behind them and said quietly, "Keep the men moving. Keep them closed up."

"Yes, sir," answered the trooper.

Tim kneed Midnight on into the fringe of woodland. He gave the mare her head since he could not see anything anyway. He breathed a sigh of relief when she finally carried him into the expanse of orchard.

"It's all open country from here on, sir," he said to Mosby, who rode up beside him.

"How far to the first battery?" asked the chief, as he pulled his grey to a halt.

"About three miles, sir. The others are about five hundred yards apart from there on."

Mosby turned to a sergeant. "Get the officers up to the head of the column," he ordered.

Within minutes the captain and the three lieutenants were grouped around the Major. Tim moved Midnight back away from them.

"Come up here, Morgan," ordered Mosby impatiently. "I want you to hear this, too."

"Gentlemen," began the Partisan chief, "this attack must be timed exactly right to achieve success. Each of you will take twenty-five men. Morgan here will point out the batteries as we ride by. One detail will drop off at each gun. Keep your men well back out of sight. We must surprise the Yankees." He paused for a moment. "All will attack on my signal—three quick pistol shots! Are there any questions?"

"I'd like to ask young Morgan a question, sir," said the Captain.

"Go ahead."

The Captain turned and faced Tim. "How do we know you'll stop precisely behind each gun?" he asked.

"If you'd like, sir," said Tim, "we can dismount and I'll take you up close enough to see them."

"Fair enough," replied the captain. He turned back to Mosby. "With your permission, sir, I would like him to do just that."

"Very well," said the Partisan chief. "Morgan will take you close enough to avoid mistakes. . . . But now, we must get on. We have less than two hours to get into position. General Stuart will start crossing the ford at dawn. Those guns must be in our hands by then!" He turned to Tim and told him, "Take the lead again, Morgan."

Tim kept Midnight at a fast walk through the orchard. When he reached the road where he and Slaughter had narrowly avoided the Federal troop, he stopped and studied it carefully. The rain had let up some, but it was still a black night. With the hundred horses behind, he could never hear a Yankee troop on the road. Tim glanced questioningly at Mosby.

"We'll go on," said the Partisan chief. He removed his hat and swung it in an arc to shake off the water. "Nobody but a Ranger would be out on a night like this anyway," he added dryly.

Even though the night was dark, Tim felt nakedly visible to Yankee eyes when he crossed into the open meadow. Off to the left he could make out the wooded hill holding the Union batteries. He glanced to the rear and saw that the column had closed up again. If the Federals had any vedettes this side of the batteries, they were sure to be seen.

"How much farther?" asked Mosby brusquely.

"We're almost to the first battery, sir," answered Tim as he looked over the hill to the south. He reined Midnight in slightly. "We can leave off the first detail here."

Mosby's hand went up. Tim could hear the column come to a halt as the hoarse whispers of the sergeants worked back down the line. A lieutenant walked his horse to the head of the battalion.

"This it?" he asked Tim.

"Yes, sir," the boy answered. He pointed to one tree taller than the others, on top of the hill. "The gun is just to the left of that tall tree."

"How much time will you need to take the lieutenant up close enough for a quick look?" asked Mosby.

"About fifteen minutes, sir," answered Tim.

"You have ten," said Mosby. "Get going."

Tim slid off Midnight and handed the reins to the nearest trooper. "Follow me, sir," he said to the lieutenant and headed for the wooded hill at a fast walk. Although he was confident of the location of the first battery, it crossed his mind that he might possibly be wrong. He began to worry. Mosby would skin him alive if he missed any of the guns, especially the first. Tim increased his pace, and behind him he could hear the lieutenant's boots sucking at muddy ground with every step he took.

At the bottom of the hill he paused and motioned the officer to stop behind him. Tim listened carefully, but heard no sound except rain dripping from trees on the hillside.

"We better move up slowly," he whispered. "If it's all right with you, I think we'd better take off our oil-skins. Seems to me they make a lot of noise when they rustle."

"Right," the lieutenant agreed and peeled off his rain cape. "Leave 'em here. We'll pick them up on the way back." He folded the cape and placed it on the ground beside Tim's. "Hurry," he said impatiently.

Tim moved up the hillside as quietly as possible. He'd say this for the lieutenant, he made practically no noise in the woods. Just before the two Rangers reached the crest of the hill, Tim stopped again and pointed to a dull glow ahead.

"That's their fire," he whispered.

The lieutenant moved forward a few paces and studied the surrounding terrain as best he could in the darkness. Satisfied at length, he retraced his steps.

He complimented Tim in a low voice. "Good boy! The gun's there all right, and with this cover we can be on 'em before they know there's anyone around. Let's get back."

The Ranger officer set a fast pace back to his waiting chief. Tim followed with a feeling of exhilaration. He thanked his lucky star that Slaughter had insisted they crawl close enough actually to see the batteries when they had made their scouting trip.

Mosby, impatient for their return, had walked his horse in their direction. "Was it there?" he demanded.

"Yes, sir," answered the lieutenant, puffing. "Right where Morgan said it would be."

"Good," answered Mosby with satisfaction. "Get your detail together and try to find cover for the next hour or so. Mount up, Morgan," he ordered, "and show me the next gun."

Tim led the rest of the troops forward. When he established his bearings for the next battery, he stopped. Mosby checked his grey. "This the second gun?" he asked.

"Yes, sir," replied Tim. "Just to the left of that saddle-back." He pointed to a place where the crest of the hill dipped slightly.

"You sure?" Mosby demanded.

"Yes, sir."

Mosby pointed out the spot to a second officer who rode up at that moment for orders. "There's your gun."

"You want Morgan to take me up for a look?" the Ranger lieutenant asked.

"No," answered the chief decisively. "He was right about the first battery. He'll be right about this one. Hold your men here."

Thanks to Slaughter's careful scout, Tim had no difficulty spotting the remaining two batteries. When the fourth and last detail had been posted, Mosby ordered Tim to follow him as he rode back down the line of four details to check their positions for the last time.

When they returned, Tim began to wonder whether the wiry little leader was ever at rest for a minute. As for himself, he felt as if he had been in the saddle for days on end. His clothing, wet through by this time, began to chafe. Rain began again and little trickles of water poured off his wide-brimmed hat. He glanced at Mosby, whose dashing plume now drooped forlornly over his hat as the Major sat his mount, watching the eastern sky for the first grey light of dawn.

Suddenly the Major raised a hand. Troopers dismounted and handed their reins to several horse holders detailed earlier. Mosby moved forward. The Rangers automatically spread out in a skirmish line and crept towards the Yankee guns.

Tim felt his pulse quicken. He gripped his Spencer tightly in one hand. This was it!

CHAPTER ELEVEN

THE YOUNGEST CORPORAL

When Major Mosby reached the foot of the hill, he stopped and waited until the line of Rangers had straightened out at the edge of the wooded area. Then he motioned his men forward again. Tim, following close on the Major's heels, heard a nearby Ranger slip on the muddy hillside and fall heavily.

"Silence!" Mosby hissed.

The luckless Ranger muttered a low, disgruntled oath and moved forward again.

Now that dawn was breaking, Tim hoped the Yankees hadn't decided to put vedettes out in the woods. As the grey streaks on the horizon became brighter, he began to think of the Yankee gun's crew on top of the hill. Soon they would be getting up. Once again Tim felt his stomach tighten.

As Mosby climbed steadily upwards, it seemed that he almost intended to crawl right into the gun clearing before he stopped. . . . But the Partisan chief merely wanted to get a good view of the battery. With only meagre underbrush to screen him, he sat on the muddy ground and studied the emplacement.

Tim cradled his rifle and hid behind a bush. He saw only four small tents and one sleepy Yankee gathering firewood from a small pile. Yawning, the bluecoat stirred up the embers, cursing because the wet wood was slow to ignite. As he knelt down to blow the embers into a blaze, a brief wave of pity for the unsuspecting soldier swept over Tim.

From the camp beyond the hill, the distant sound of a bugle floated up to the waiting Rangers. Mosby tensed, looked around the woods, and raised his Colt. Tim braced himself for a quick charge.

Wham! Wham! Wham!

Mosby's big Colt slammed out three deafening shots. A bloodcurdling chorus of Rebel yells shattered the morning stillness as the woods exploded with the noise of their guns. The attack was on!

Tim saw the soldier at the fire spring to his feet, eyes filled with terror, as the Partisans broke into the clearing. He raised his hands as high as he could get them. Artillerymen poured out of the tents.

Mosby ran forward, a Colt in each hand.

"Take 'em prisoner!" the Major yelled and headed for the nearest tent. Union soldiers poured out into the open in various states of undress. At the sight of the grey-clad Rangers, most of them quickly raised their hands. One braver, or perhaps more foolhardy than the rest, reached for a rifle near the tent entrance.

Mosby steadied his Colt on the man's forehead.

"Touch that rifle and you're a dead man," he warned.

The soldier took another look at Mosby, then slowly raised his hands along with the rest.

"Take four men to guard these prisoners," the Major ordered. "The rest of you clear the gun for action. See if you can depress it on the camp below."

Tim ran with the others to the gun. The Rangers threw their weight into the job and soon had the murderous weapon rolled forward into position. They found, however, that the gun could not be depressed sufficiently to fire on the Yankees below.

"There comes Stuart!" yelled a Ranger, pointing towards the Virginia bank.

Tim saw a column of grey-clad cavalry, guidons snapping in the breeze, come pounding down the bank into the river at the ford. They had carbines in hand, butts resting against their hips as the first mounts splashed into the shallow water. Both up and down river additional cavalry broke from cover to take the ford at a gallop.

Below, Yankees grouped for a defence of the crossing. They ran across the single bridge over the canal at this point and took up positions along the river-bank. Bugles rang out and a wave of musket fire swept the river. As more fire lashed out from the Blue lines, now under good cover, empty saddles appeared here and there among the ranks of the Grey. Tim heard the deep boom of a cannon to the south and saw a crater appear in the ground just behind the Yankee line of defence.

"That's number three battery!" cried Mosby. "Our boys have it in action! Roll this gun over the hill and jam it in the trees! That'll give us the line of fire we want!"

The Rangers heaved on the wheels and rolled the gun to the crest of the hill. With a yell they pushed it on over. It slammed up against two trees to come to a ground-shaking halt. Now that they had the gun on a slope, it would range on the camp below.

Out of the corner of his eye Tim caught a movement

on the path leading up from the Yankee camp. Suddenly a young bugler broke into the clearing and shouted breathlessly, "The Colonel wants to know . . . !" When he caught sight of Confederates around the gun, his mouth dropped open in astonishment. He stared unbelievingly for a minute, then screamed, "Rebels!"

"Grab that boy!" shouted Mosby.

Tim lunged at the bugler and pinioned his arms.

"Lemme go!" screamed the youngster. He broke one arm free and grabbed the bugle hanging by a yellow rope over his shoulder. He twisted in Tim's arms and brought the bugle down in a smashing blow on the young Ranger's head. "Lemme go!" he screamed again.

The blow brought tears to Tim's eyes. He grabbed the youngster's arm and twisted it roughly behind his back.

"Quiet down, you fool," growled Tim. "You want to get shot?"

"Rebels!" the boy screamed at the top of his voice.

"Quiet!" snapped Mosby.

"Quiet yourself, you rotten Rebel!" yelled the boy.

Mosby's eyes turned cold as ice. "Tie him up," he ordered Tim. "Gag him if necessary."

"No you don't, you——"

Tim slapped his hand quickly over the boy's mouth and dragged him back away from the crest of the hill. With the help of another Ranger, he tied the kicking youngster's hands and feet.

By the time Tim got back to the gun, the Rangers had it firing. Below, the Yankee camp had become a scene of utter confusion. With the murderous attack on their rear, the Union defenders began to waver on the defence line. Stuart's cavalry galloped relentlessly on in spite of their losses. The sound of Confederate bugles mingled with the wild Rebel yells of the attacking horsemen. When the grey cavalry hit the Maryland side, they spread out and charged the line of defenders on the top of the bank.

The Union line broke. Soldiers dashed for the bridge in a mad scramble to cross the canal. Some got across and blue-clad officers whipped together pockets of defence. Stuart's horsemen hit the swirling humanity on the single bridge, rolled over and rode down the remaining defenders. One by one all pockets of resistance were either captured or wiped out. The camp was in Confederate hands.

Satisfied that he could do no more for Stuart's cavalry, Mosby turned back from the scene below and approached the prisoners. He looked the sullen group over carefully his eyes finally coming to rest on the young bugler tied hand and foot.

"Untie his feet, Morgan," he directed.

Tim knelt beside the youngster and untied his feet. He put his hands under the boy's arms and helped him to stand.

When the boy was once again on his feet, he looked Tim in the eye, then deliberately kicked him in the shin.

"Ouch!" yelled Tim as he backed away, rubbing his shinbone.

"That's enough of that!" snapped Mosby angrily. "Behave yourself!"

A Ranger took a step forward. "Maybe I ought to tan his bottom, Major," he offered grimly.

Mosby waved the trooper back and faced the rest of

the prisoners. "Your camp is now in our hands," he said. "You will be taken to General Stuart's headquarters and be given an opportunity to sign a parole."

"I ain't gonna sign no parole," growled the defiant young bugler.

Mosby stared at the boy coldly. "Young man, my patience is wearing thin. You will speak only when spoken to."

Tears of rage welled up in the boy's eyes. Tim felt a quick pang of sympathy for him.

"Take 'em down the hill, sergeant," Mosby ordered.

The sergeant started to herd the prisoners single file down the trail towards camp. The young bugler stood his ground.

"I ain't gonna take orders from no Rebel," he growled sullenly.

The sergeant raised his hand to clout the youngster.

"Hold it, sergeant," said the Partisan chief. He pointed to two of the Federal soldiers. "You two pick him up and carry him," he ordered.

The two Federals took hold of the youngster, but the youth shook them off, turned and headed down the trail, head held high.

Mosby's stern eyes followed the stubborn young boy. Finally he broke into a grin. "I would say he's about the fightin'est Yankee the 43rd ever ran into." He sobered as he stared at the retreating figure. "God help the Confederacy if all Yankees were as fearless." He swung around abruptly. "Back to the horses, men. We'll ride into camp."

General Stuart greeted Mosby with real enthusiasm

when he rode up at the head of his 43rd Battalion. When the Partisan chief dismounted, Stuart grabbed his hand and shook it warmly. "John, you've done it again!" he said. He then addressed his staff officers. "Gentlemen, here is the man who paved the way for our attack and reduced defensive action to a minimum." The General turned back to Mosby, then caught sight of the waiting Rangers. He walked down the line of mounted men, looking them over proudly. Finally, about midway along the column he stopped. "Men!" he shouted. "I'm proud of you. You're a credit to the South!"

Tim saw the hardened Rangers grin shyly, embarrassed by the praise. A sergeant near the head of the column raised his broad-brimmed hat, and the Rangers gave a mighty cheer for the popular general. Stuart, pleased with the spontaneous salute, waved his own plumed hat as the battalion rode on to a bivouac area.

"Fine bunch of men, John," he said admiringly.

"Thank you, sir," said Mosby. "They have a few rough edges, but they're pretty handy in a fight." He hesitated for a minute, then asked, "Did your men find any prisoners in the camp, sir? One of my Rangers was taken night before last."

General Stuart motioned to an aide. "Check with the provost marshal and find out if we recaptured any of our men."

"Yes, sir." The young officer saluted and hurried away.

"This man is important to you?" he inquired sharply.

"Yes, General," replied Mosby. He outlined briefly

how Slaughter and Tim had scouted the Yankee camp.

"Morgan," said Stuart musingly. "Is he with you now?"

"Yes, sir."

"Send him to me, John. I'd like to tell him myself how valuable I consider his contribution."

"General Stuart wants to see me?" asked Tim incredulously.

"That's right," said the staff officer. "Come on. Don't keep him waiting."

"Yes, sir," mumbled Tim in confusion. He glanced down at his muddied uniform.

"Never mind your looks," said the officer. "The General won't care about that," he added kindly. "Come on."

Tim followed the cavalry officer through the camp, at a loss to know why he had been singled out by the General. Suddenly the thought occurred to him that Stuart had changed his mind about Midnight and had decided he wanted her. His heart sank. Anything but that!

Tim saw the General, flanked by his staff, studying a map. Officers always seemed to be looking at maps. He waited until Stuart looked up, then saluted smartly.

"Trooper Morgan reporting, sir," he said in a quavering voice.

Stuart's eyes twinkled. "At ease, trooper." He looked the boy over curiously. "Haven't I seen you before?"

"Yes, sir," replied Tim quaking, and reminded the General of his visit with Mosby.

"Oh, yes," said Stuart. "I remember now. You have that fine black mare." He thought for a minute. "Midnight, you called her."

"That's right, sir," replied Tim, certain now that the General meant to take his horse.

"How is she?"

"Fine, sir."

"Good," replied Stuart. "Take care of her. She's a fine animal." He suddenly became serious. "Major Mosby has described your outstanding achievements of the last few days. Your contribution has perhaps been far greater than you imagine."

Tim flushed at the outspoken praise.

"Thank you—sir," he stammered.

"As an old soldier, your father will be proud of your service," said the General. "I have instructed Major Mosby to write and tell him that your actions will be mentioned in my dispatches to General Lee."

Tim just stared at the General in astonishment. He couldn't believe a general would go to all that trouble for a common soldier. Finally he managed to remember his manners. "It'll make Pa very happy, sir," he said quietly.

Stuart looked at the boy with a twinkle in his eyes. "Your conduct merits such a report, Corporal."

Tim gazed astonished at the General.

"Yes," said Stuart with a smile. "I said 'Corporal.' " He turned to his staff. "And I suspect, gentlemen, the youngest corporal in the Confederate Army." To Tim he continued, "You may go now, Corporal. The sutler should be able to provide you with your chevrons." Then he added with a chuckle, "But the way Major

Mosby keeps you Rangers in the saddle, I doubt whether you'll ever find time to sew them on."

Tim saluted and walked proudly away from headquarters. When he reached the cover of the still-standing Yankee tents, he broke into a dead run and raced back to the camp area of the 43rd Battalion. Just as he reached the camp-fire, Tim spotted Hank Slaughter, surrounded by a group of Rangers.

"Hank! Hank!" Tim shouted. "You all right?" He ran up to the sergeant.

"You bet I am, Tim," Slaughter replied with a happy grin. "I was sure hopin' you fellows'd get here before the Yanks sent me on to prison."

Tim looked down at Hank's ankle.

"Just a sprain," he explained. "Doc says I can ride if I take care of it." He reached up and fingered his scalp carefully. "That Yankee sure clouted me with a pistol butt, though. Good thing I got a hard head."

"Safest place to hit you, Hank," yelled one Ranger laughingly. "Reckon he had to throw the pistol away."

Slaughter took the ribbing good-naturedly, but before long the tired Ranger group dwindled away as the men headed for a soft spot to catch a nap.

"The Major told me how well you placed the battalion last night, Tim," said Slaughter when the others had left. "I'm right proud of you."

"I just took 'em there, Hank, that's all," said Tim. "I tried to remember all you told me."

"Looks like you did a pretty good job of it," said the other. "But look. We can talk later. The 43rd's headin' out in two hours. You better grab some sleep."

"Holy mackerel! Two hours!" exclaimed Tim. He grinned broadly and added, "Guess the General's right."

"What's that?"

"I'll tell you later, Hank," Tim answered evasively. "I better get a nap, like you said."

CHAPTER TWELVE

WAR CAN BE WASTE

THE 43RD drove relentlessly north through the rich farm land of Maryland. Acting as scouts for General Stuart's brigade, now miles to the rear, the Rangers kept a wary eye open for Yankee troops. Armies, both Confederate and Federal, were on the move all over three states. Mosby swung his Rangers east on a feint towards the Union capital of Washington and laughed when he heard that two companies of Union cavalry had been detached to hunt him down.

Maryland farmers, with little or no warning of the Confederate move north into their state, fled with livestock, when they could, or tried to hide their possessions from the Grey foraging parties swooping down on them. As the days wore on, Mosby sent an ever-increasing supply of horses, mules, and cattle back to Virginia. Determined to deplete the rich farm lands as the Federals had ravaged the South, he kept the 43rd in the saddle until the men could sleep sitting their mounts. At length the tough Partisan chief recognised the battalion's need for a rest and went into camp on a mountain side near the Pennsylvania-Maryland border. There the men slaughtered beef and had their first really good meal in a week.

Tim lay on the ground, head resting in his saddle, and stared at the few fleecy clouds in the blue sky. He could not help thinking back over the events of the past few days; the quick raids, foraging parties looting farms and the stricken farmers standing helplessly by as they were robbed. He knew it had to be done—knew the Confederate armies must have food, but it seemed then that war was a terrible waste.

He turned his head in the saddle and studied the lean form of Sergeant Slaughter stretched out on the ground a few feet away.

"You awake, Hank?"

The other gave a satisfied groan and rolled to face the boy. "Almost. I ain't eaten that much since the end of '60."

"Where do you think the Major's headed for?" asked Tim.

"Dunno. North, I reckon," replied the other. "Acts like he's gonna go clear to New York."

"I heard there's going to be a big battle," said Tim.

"'Spec' so. The Major told one of the officers that all the armies were facin' each other up in Pennsylvania. Place called Gettysburg, or sumthin' like that."

"You figger we're going to win, Hank?" Tim asked soberly.

"I reckon." Hank raised up on one elbow. "You know, though, these blue bellies don't scare as easy as they useta. Guess they're learnin' how to fight."

"How long d'ye think it'll last?" asked Tim.

"The battle?" Hank asked absently. " 'Til one side starts runnin' away."

"No, I mean the whole war," said Tim.

"Ain't no way of tellin', I guess," Hank replied. He glanced at the boy sharply. "What's on your mind? Gettin' fed up?"

Tim hesitated for a minute. "No, it's not that. It's—well—I don't think much of a war where you go around robbin' folks that only want to live peaceably."

Hank studied the boy's troubled face shrewdly. "I see what you mean, Tim, but you gotta look at it this way. The Yankees stole everything that wasn't nailed down in Virginia, and they didn't need horses and food and such as much as we do." He paused for a moment. "I don't hold with robbin' folks either, but if it's the only way we can keep Lee's army fed—then I say the Yankees'll have to suffer.'

"I suppose so," admitted Tim reluctantly.

"Of course it's so." Then, to take the young trooper's mind off the subject, Hank sat up and reached for his boot. "Help me with this boot, will you?"

Tim knelt beside Hank and caught the boot heel gently. Slaughter had split the leather down to his instep to relieve the pressure on the still swollen ankle. The boy frowned as he slipped the leather off and noticed the swelling. He looked up as the other winced with the pain of the movement.

"You'd better tell the Major about this, Hank," Tim exclaimed. "Looks like it's swelling up again."

Slaughter touched the joint gingerly. "Hurts a mite, but a day's rest ought to take care of it."

Tim was not so sure. The ankle looked worse than it had for several days. Further conversation was cut short as a vedette broke into the camp clearing on the run. The two Rangers saw him head straight for a light canvas shelter which Mosby had ordered stretched over a small box he was using as a field desk. Mosby stood up as the man approached, and they watched him receive the report in silence. Practically every trooper in the camp had his eyes on the chief.

The camp was not kept in ignorance very long. At the conclusion of the report, Mosby motioned for all the troopers to gather near the shelter. When they had assembled, he looked them over silently. Depleted by Rangers sent south with livestock, a few casualties, and several troopers sent at Stuart's request to augment his scouts, the 43rd numbered no more than sixty effectives.

"A wagon train has been reported on the road below," the Major explained. "It's not large, but one platoon of cavalry stands guard." He looked over his tired followers. "We'll go down and capture the wagons, but we'll keep our camp here for a while. I'll take only thirty men."

The thirty raiders detailed for the job quickly saddled up.

"You ought not to go on this raid," said Tim anxiously to Slaughter, who was tightening the girth on his saddle. "Let me tell the Major about your ankle."

"You keep your mouth shut," snapped the sergeant. "I was detailed just like you, and I go, sprained ankle or no!"

Tim shrugged resignedly and swung on to Midnight's back. He spun the cylinder in his pistol and loosened the Spencer in its saddle holster. Such preparations before a raid had become automatic in the past few weeks.

Mosby led the Rangers out of the clearing at a fast trot. When they started down the mountain trail, the detail necessarily slowed down. Tim could see why

Mosby had selected the clearing for a resting place. Any attack on their camp would have to push up the narrow trail, and a handful of defenders could hold off a company.

The raiders cut the road at a point where it crossed a shallow mountain stream. Mosby posted his men up and downstream and took a dozen men down the mountain road. This meant that he intended to attack from three directions.

Tim found himself, along with Sergeant Slaughter, among the twelve men on the road with Major Mosby. They trotted on until hidden from the creek crossing by a turn in the road. Here Mosby dismounted and back-tracked on foot until he could see the place where the road dipped into the stream. He studied the terrain for a few minutes, then hurried back to his waiting Rangers.

"Morgan!" he snapped.

"Yes, sir," answered Tim.

"You saw where I was just standing." He nodded towards the turn. "Go on up there and keep out of sight. Wait until you see the Yankees crossing the creek." He paused to make sure that Tim understood. "The advance guard ought to be about fifty yards ahead of the first wagon. Wait until that wagon hits the creek, then give me a signal. You understand?"

"Yes, sir," said Tim. He reflected for a minute. "Sir, what if the advance guard leads the wagon more than fifty yards?"

"You'll have to judge the distance then," answered Mosby. "I want to round that turn at a dead run when the troopers are precisely fifty yards this side of the creek."

"Fifty yards. Yes, sir," Tim repeated.

"Give your horse to Slaughter. When we come by, you can grab her." He turned to the others. "Check your weapons. I figure they'll be here in five minutes."

Tim handed Midnight's reins to Slaughter and ran towards the turn in the road. He moved off the rutted surface into the ditch at the side and peered cautiously towards the creek. He could not hear a sound from the Rangers hidden in the creek. He waited patiently, listening to the buzzing of insects in the thick underbrush. He did not have long to wait. Muffled at first, the familiar sounds of wagoners' whips and shouts gradually increased in volume. At length, three cavalrymen at point rode into view. Tim watched them close the distance steadily. He glanced over his shoulder and saw that the Rangers were watching him closely. Again he studied the Yankee horsemen. The troopers looked alert as they rode, their eyes scanning the woods on either side. Tim saw they were wary; each blue-clad trooper rode with his carbine in hand, butt resting on his hip. As closely as he could estimate, there were twenty cavalrymen in the guard, riding by fours on the narrow road.

He saw the lead horses hit the creek. When a trooper's mount stopped and dropped its head for water, he heard a lieutenant shout angrily, "Keep closed up!" Tim glanced back at the few Rangers nervously. These were veteran Union cavalrymen up ahead.

Mosby had guessed right. The guard kept very close to fifty yards ahead of the first wagon. Soon the cavalrymen were across, and Tim watched the driver of the wagon haul back on his brake handle as his team started down the slight slope where the road dipped into the stream.

Tim raised his hand high and risked another quick look at the Rangers. They sat tense and waiting. When the front wheels of the heavily loaded wagon splashed into the water, he brought his hand down sharply.

Behind him, the Rangers spurred their mounts. Mosby swept past, reins in his teeth and a pistol in each hand. Tim grabbed for Midnight's cantle as she roared by, bounced his feet on the ground twice as she dragged him along, then swung into the saddle. By the time he found the wildly swinging stirrups, the Rebel Raiders had left him a good dozen lengths behind the last mount. He drew his pistol, leaned low over Midnight's neck and dug his heels into her flanks. He felt her lunge forward to close the distance.

The two bodies of horsemen came together with a tremendous crash. Surprised the Yankees might be, and with no time to get set for a countercharge, yet it was only the momentum of the Rebel horsemen that drove the head of the Union troop back. The troopers in the rear gave no ground but surged forward to help the head of the column.

As Rebel pistols spat death, Tim saw the bright blades of Union sabres flash in the sun. And then Midnight carried him into the centre of the milling turmoil. A Yankee trooper swung a vicious cut at Tim's head. He ducked low in the saddle, and the blade swished dangerously close. He saw a horse, screaming its protest, break for the underbrush. A lifeless Yankee, his foot caught in the stirrup, bounced along with it. There were empty Ranger saddles, too. Tim could feel the pressure of the rallying Yankees as he cleared his sabre in time to take a murderous slash close to the hilt of his blade. The blow all but numbed his whole arm. Slaughter cleared his way to the boy's side, and the pressure eased momentarily.

Suddenly wild Rebel yells roared up from the rear of the Yankee guard. As Blue cavalrymen in the rear of the action wheeled to meet this new threat, Tim heard Mosby scream, "Drive 'em!"

For a moment there was confusion and uncertainty among the Yankees. Tim heard a blue-clad sergeant rally the defence with vivid profanity. Desperately, the trapped Yankees tried to cut their way clear.

Mosby's high voice rose above the din of battle. "Surrender, Yanks! You're trapped!"

Gradually the noise lessened, and soon the surrounded Yankee troopers sat sullenly between the two Rebel forces, their hands held high in the air. Quickly the Rangers disarmed the prisoners. Leaving a small guard, Mosby collected the rest of his Partisans and headed for the distant sound of firing towards the rear of the train.

As Tim passed down the wagon train, he noted that every seat was empty. The drivers had dived into the underbrush at the first pistol shot.

Mosby led his men into the fight with the rear guard at a full gallop. When the Federals saw this reinforcement, those remaining in their saddles quickly yielded. These were quickly herded back to the creek crossing.

The raid had been costly, more costly than Mosby had expected. He counted his losses grimly. Another hot engagement like this one and he would have few effectives left. He ordered the tarpaulins taken off two of the wagons and had the wounded, Blue and Grey alike, laid out. Ten Rangers were unfit for further service, and five more would never ride again. Federal losses were even heavier. Sixteen blue-clad troopers were seriously wounded; nine had given their lives for the Union.

Among the dead was a Federal lieutenant. Mosby saluted the brave officer gravely and detailed a squad of prisoners as a burial party. Rangers and Federals alike pitched in to ease the suffering of the wounded.

Mosby made a quick inspection of the wagons. He swept back a canvas cover over some boxes. Printed on the side were the words, "SULPHATE OF QUINA." He threw the cover farther back and read the next label, "MORPHIA." The Partisan chief glanced at the Rangers with him.

"No wonder they fought for this train," he said with satisfaction. "These ten wagons are worth a fortune! General Lee will be pleased, very pleased."

The Rangers spread out through the woods and soon rounded up the frightened civilian drivers. To most of them, the name Mosby represented a legend, a legend that chilled their very bones, to be sure; throughout the North the Partisan chief was depicted as a barbarous murderer.

In the meantime, Tim kept busy ministering to the needs of the wounded Rangers. Both Partisans and Yankees freely used bandages and medicines from the supply wagons. The work kept him busy for the better part of an hour. At last, when he had done what he could for his own friends, he sauntered over to where the wounded Federals lay.

"Did you get everything you need?" he asked a soldier who was working over a Federal sergeant, cleaning a nasty thigh wound.

The Union soldier glanced at the boy in annoyance. "We'll make out, Reb——"

"Mither of God!" the wounded sergeant's voice exploded. " 'Tis the Morgan lad himself!"

Tim stared at the prisoner in astonishment. "Murphy!" he cried. He looked at the regimental device on the soldiers' jackets. "I didn't know this was the 5th New York!" He knelt beside the wounded trooper. "How do you feel?" he asked anxiously.

"I'll not be doin' a jig fer awhile," the Yankee sergeant answered, glancing ruefully at his wounded leg. He stared at the boy appraisingly. " 'Tis glad I am, lad, to find ye in a proper uniform."

Tim flushed. "Is there anything I can get you, Sergeant?" he asked.

"You know this man, Morgan?"

Tim looked over his shoulder to see Mosby standing above him, his face stern.

Tim jumped up quickly. "Yes, sir. This is Sergeant Murphy of the 5th New York."

"So?" queried the Partisan chief.

"He had the sentry post on Little River Turnpike, sir," explained Tim. "He's the one that had the fight with Bull Ruffing."

The Major's eyes showed remembrance of Tim's

experience on the turnpike. He stared at the wounded trooper curiously. "Your men fought well, Sergeant," he said.

Murphy returned the stare with a level look. "Thank ye, Major."

"Are you the senior sergeant of the platoon?" asked Mosby.

"Yes, sir," answered Murphy promptly.

"Then I'll explain what I have in mind," said Mosby. "Stay where you are!" he ordered as Murphy winced with the pain of trying to sit up. "All of our wounded need help," he continued, "and yours as well. The wagon train is ours. I intend to send it to our people. The wagons will carry our wounded back, and I also intend to send your casualties along. We'll leave you Yankees in good hands somewhere along the line." Mosby looked around the group of Yankee wounded. "Men, I intend to send you along with the wagons and will make every effort to get medical attention for you. But," he demanded, "you will all sign a parole first."

The Federal wounded stared sullenly at Mosby. Not one of them spoke.

"That sounds fair enough to me, Major." Murphy's eyes swept the helpless prisoners. "We'll all sign."

Although Mosby proposed to let the wounded accompany the train, he did not extend this sympathy to those Yankees who could walk or ride. These he intended to take back to camp with him and hold. Even those who signed paroles must go along until the train was well clear.

Valuable as were the contents of the wagons, Mosby could spare no more than four Rangers for a train guard.

Learning of Slaughter's continued trouble with his ankle, he placed the veteran sergeant in command. Slaughter requested Tim for the detail. The boy did not know whether to be glad or not, but, after thinking it over, he realised that Slaughter perhaps wanted to spare him any more foraging details.

With usual Ranger efficiency, the train was soon under way. Partisan and Federal wounded were laid on top of the stores and made as comfortable as was possible. One wagon yielded a load of hospital blankets, and these helped cushion the rough ride. Tim had Slaughter put Murphy in the first wagon where the boy could look out for him, since he rode at point with the Ranger sergeant.

"So that's the Yankee you didn't crack down on back on the turnpike raid," said Slaughter.

"That's him," replied Tim. "I don't reckon I could shoot him even if he is a Yankee."

Hank glanced back at the first wagon where Murphy, propped up on the stores, watched the two of them riding up ahead. "He's a good man, all right," he conceded. "After that Yankee lieutenant got shot, it was Murphy who rallied the rest. Reckon if he hadn't taken one in the thigh, things would've been tougher yet." He turned his attention to the road ahead. "Tim," he said, "we got ourselves a long haul to that farmhouse where the Major said to leave the Yanks. Suppose you ride back along the wagons and make sure they're keeping closed up."

"Right," Tim acknowledged and wheeled Midnight. He trotted back down the line, cautioning each of the civilian drivers to keep their wagons moving. For the most part, the wagoners were too scared of their Ranger guard to utter a word. They merely cracked their whips when the boy spoke.

When he reached the end of the line, he saw John White, one of the two Ranger rear guard, spur his horse and join him at a gallop.

"What's up?" asked White, ready for instant action.

"Hank wants to be sure the wagons keep movin'," Tim explained. "He wants to reach the farmhouse by dark."

"They'll move," answered the trooper grimly. "Tell Hank to keep the first wagon movin' along. The others'll follow if we have to build a fire under 'em."

By late afternoon the road levelled off some. Hank stood up in his stirrups and studied the valley ahead.

"We oughta be comin' to that fork in the road the Major told us about right soon," he said. "That farm should be just beyond the fork." He settled back in his saddle. "Suppose you meander on ahead and take a look. But be careful. If we're gonna see any Yanks, they'll have 'em posted at the fork."

Tim nodded and spurred Midnight into a trot. He rode for a few minutes, then stopped to listen. Slowly he walked the mare forward until he saw a division of the road ahead. He stopped again and carefully studied the dividing lanes. Seeing no sign of the enemy, once again he touched his mare on the flank and approached at a fast trot. Once there, he saw that both roads were deserted. Out of curiosity he decided to swerve right and see if the farmhouse was really there.

He had gone but a few hundred yards when he sighted the roof of a house through the trees. He left the road, tethered Midnight well back in the woods, and pushed his way through the underbrush for a better look.

The clearing around the house was ample for all ten wagons. In the rear he saw a barn and several outbuildings. A thin wisp of smoke rose leisurely from a rock-and-clay chimney on one side of the house, and although there was no one in evidence outside, it was obvious that someone occupied the place.

Taking care that no watchful gaze was on him, Tim ran back to the tethered mare, mounted, and headed for the wagon train.

"We'll have to chance it," said Slaughter when Tim had explained the layout. "No sign of Yankee horse around the farm?"

"No livestock of any kind," replied Tim.

Slaughter glanced back at the wagons anxiously. "Go speed 'em up, Tim. I want to get 'em down there quick." He glanced at the sun, now low in the western sky.

Fifteen minutes later the first driver turned his team off the road into the tree-sheltered farmyard. Slaughter and Tim rode up to the porch of the house.

"Hullo!" called Slaughter. "Anyone t'home?"

The door opened and a grim-faced woman walked out, a shotgun in her hand. She stood staring angrily at the two Rangers.

"Git!" she spat, hatred in her eyes. "We ain't got nothin' left fer ye t' take." She brought the shotgun up menacingly.

"Git, I say!" she demanded.

"Ma'am," said Slaughter with determination, "we ain't askin' nothin' for ourselves. We got a load of badly wounded men, Yanks and Confederates both. We want to camp here for the night."

Tim saw the muzzle of the shotgun waver as the woman stared suspiciously at the wagons.

Her eyes swung back to the two Rangers and looked them over carefully. "I'll take a look fer myself," she said and started down the steps. "I ain't sayin' ye kin stay, though," she warned.

Hank winked at Tim and walked his horse behind the woman as she peered into the wagons. When at length she satisfied herself that the Ranger sergeant spoke the truth she looked up at him sternly.

"One night," she said decisively. "Hear me? One night only! Then ye'll be off!"

Slaughter nodded. "Yes, ma'am," he agreed meekly.

CHAPTER THIRTEEN

BUSHWHACKERS

SERGEANT SLAUGHTER put the drivers to work building fires. He had to risk their trying to make a break for the woods, but realised they would probably disappear during the night anyway if they weren't watched carefully. He posted two Rangers on the road to cover both approaches to the farm. When the fires were roaring, the wounded were moved on to the ground, close to the comforting warmth of burning logs.

Some of the injured had suffered greatly during the day. Tim made rounds with a bucket of water and a tin cup, so that the men might quench their terrible thirst. Out of the corner of his eye, Tim saw a movement on the porch, where the woman stood gazing down at the wounded soldiers. She hesitated briefly, then moved down the steps and walked quickly over to Tim.

"I reckon maybe I kin help some," she said. After looking about, she spied a young trooper lying on his back, face contorted with pain. She knelt beside him, and, after gingerly opening his shirt, peered at his gaping shoulder wound.

"Git some water bilin'," she demanded. "You got any medicine?"

"Ten wagons full," Tim told her with a nod towards the parked train.

She looked at him and snorted, "What do men know

about the ailin'?" She rose, then strode to the bottom of the steps and shouted:

"Sarah! Louisa! Git out here and help me."

Cautiously the front door opened, and two girls about Tim's own age peered timidly from the porch.

Tim stared at them, astonished, wondering where they had been hidden.

"Come, come!" their mother said impatiently. Then she shoved Tim in the back and added, "Don't just stand there. Git around to the back of the house and fetch me two big iron pots."

"Yes, ma'am," Tim said and hurried to do her bidding.

When he returned, Hank was also taking orders from the woman. The wagoners were hustling about, responding to her directions faster and more willingly than they did for Slaughter. Apparently she had suggested that a "fittin' meal" be prepared, for several of the drivers were busy unloading food from one of the Yankee wagons, while others piled additional logs on the ground. The camp took on a meaningful, bustling air, and even the wounded began to look better.

As Tim approached, one of the girls pointed to a fire and told him to set a pot on the log supports.

"Will that be all right, Miss——?" he asked, after centring the pot over the flame.

"I'm Sarah," said the girl abruptly. "That will be good enough." She turned quickly away and busied herself with preparing food.

Tim watched as she talked and laughed with the drivers, who outdid one another to be of assistance. It seemed to Tim that for grown men they were acting mighty childish just because she was a pretty girl. Uncommonly pretty, he was forced to admit. In the gathering dusk, firelight added sparkle to her long dark hair and accentuated her piquant, saucy face.

Briefly, the time and place receded, and it seemed that only he and the girl were standing in the flickering light. Suddenly his reverie was shattered when a voice behind called out:

"Don't just stand there. Find something to do!"

It was the mother.

Tim jumped at the harsh tones and flushed when some of the wounded snickered. "Yes, ma'am," he muttered and went off to look for Hank.

He found the sergeant at the wagon train searching for bandages.

"You better give me some chore before that lady turns her shotgun on me," said Tim peevishly.

"You mean, Miz McCarthy?" Hank chuckled. "She sure did take charge."

"I'll say she did," said Tim with a backward glance towards the fires. "I don't think she likes us much, though."

"I reckon we ain't give her much reason fer likin' us," answered Slaughter. "Our boys drove off all her livestock a few days back. Her husband's with the army up Gettysburg way—Union Army at that."

"I didn't know," said Tim. "Reckon I wouldn't favour the South either."

"Don't guess you would," agreed Slaughter. "Here." He handed Tim a pile of bandages and lint. "Better get these over there 'fore she comes after us."

Tim made his way back to the largest fire, where Mrs.

McCarthy centred her activities. She saw Tim approaching.

"Sarah," she called. "Let Louisa git on with the cookin'. C'mere and help me." She turned to Tim. "You keep right behind us so's we kin have bandages handy." She looked around the yard. "Reckon I'd better change 'em all t' make sure they're clean."

Tim stood, holding the bandages, while the two women went about their duties. When either called for lint or dressing, he moved quickly to where he was needed. To his surprise, the girl worked with the same calm efficiency as her mother. He enjoyed watching her and once, when she motioned for a dressing, he moved quickly and dropped to one knee beside her. She murmured words of encouragement to the wounded man, while deftly replacing the old dressing.

"Sarah," he said, half-aloud. "That's a pretty name."

"*Miss* Sarah to you, Rebel!" she snapped, and, with a swish of her skirts, moved on to the next man.

It was on the tip of Tim's tongue to make an angry remark when he saw one of the Rangers vedette ride into the yard with a strange horseman. They halted well away from the centre of the camp, and the Ranger called Slaughter.

Tim put down the remainder of the dressings and headed for the two.

"Better hear what this feller has to say, Hank," said the vedette as Tim and the sergeant walked up.

By the seal on his saddle-bags, Tim could see the stranger was a Confederate courier. His horse, foam-flecked and heaving, could hardly stand.

"Who are you?" asked Hank.

"Name's Johnson," said the man wearily. "I'm a courier for the 1st Virginia." He glanced at Hank's chevrons. "If you're in charge here, I sure hope you can let me have a fresh horse."

Hank looked him over carefully. "Can and will, soldier," he said. "You better set a spell and eat. Looks like you been on the road fer a long time."

"I have. Since day before yesterday I ain't been outa that saddle but three times."

"What's the hurry?"

Johnson looked around the camp, dismounted and motioned the Rangers to come closer. "Guess you ain't heard about Gettysburg."

"What about it?" asked Hank.

"We took an awful lickin'," said the courier. "But then the Yanks took an awful lickin' too. Don't really know who got the worst of it, 'cept General Lee and all his army's headin' back south again." At Hank's alarmed expression, he went on, "The Yanks ain't chasin' him though. They got a bellyful too."

"Is the army behind you?" asked Hank.

"Most of 'em are west o' here."

"You know this country?" Slaughter asked.

"Middlin'," the soldier replied. "Got a pretty good map if you'd like to see it." He glanced at the wagons. "What's in 'em?"

When Hank told him, the man's eyes lighted up. "The General would send you a brigade for an escort if he knew it. He's gonna need a powerful lot of that stuff for his casualties."

"Where's General Stuart's command?" asked Tim.

The courier eyed him cautiously. "Stuart ain't very

popular right now," he said. "Seems he was up north and didn't get back in time to help Lee—so some say. . . . You fellers part of Stuart's outfit?"

"43rd Battalion," answered Tim.

"Rangers, eh?" He glanced at the feathers in the Partisans' pinned-up hats. "Shoulda guessed it right off." He looked longingly at the fire. "Now if you'll give me a cup of coffee and a fresh horse I'll be gettin' on."

"Right away," said Hank, and taking the man's arm started to lead him to the fire. He stopped abruptly and faced the hungry soldier. "I'd rather you don't say anything about Gettysburg," he said. "We got both Yanks and our own wounded here. Our boys don't need any more bad news."

"They won't hear it from me," promised the courier.

Within fifteen minutes the visitor had eaten, changed his saddle and was off again. Tim noticed the curious stares of both Rangers and Yankee wounded, but Slaughter merely explained that the stranger was a cavalryman trying to rejoin his regiment.

As the courier was about to leave, he drew Slaughter and Tim aside. "Let me show you the quickest way to make contact with the Confederate main body." He drew a map out of his pocket and explained, "Our army's retreatin' to the west o' here. The Yanks are movin' south, to your east." He traced a thin line on the map. "You'd best keep on down this road for about five miles and then take this old road west across the mountains. The pass is about here——" He indicated a spot on the paper. "Once through, you'll be in the next valley and ought to see our troops."

"How bad's that mountain pass?" asked Slaughter.

"You kin get the wagons through," the courier said, "if it don't rain. And look," he added, "I wouldn't waste any time gettin' out o' here. There's bushwhackers all over this country between the two armies."

"Bushwhackers?" asked Tim.

"Deserters, cut-throats and worse from both armies," explained the courier. "Folks just to the north o' here bin wiped out by 'em."

"How far north?" asked Slaughter.

"Mebbe ten miles!" said the other. He glanced at the wagons. "They'd give a lot to get their hands on that medicine. Sumpin' they could sell right easy." He swung on to his horse. "I'll tell the first unit I see you're on your way. Could be they'll send you some more help. Thanks for the meal."

After the courier had galloped out of the yard, Slaughter turned to Tim.

"Them gangs could cause us trouble," he said. "We got maybe four or five wounded who could handle a gun if they had to, but that still leaves us mighty short-handed."

"How about the Yankees?" asked Tim.

"No, siree," said Hank. "They might get ideas!"

Darkness had fallen quickly in the valley, and Tim could barely make out the outlines of the mountains on either side of the valley.

"Think I oughta warn the vedettes?" asked Tim, staring uneasily into the darkness.

"Right away," said Hank. "I told White to go up to the fork of the roads. Go tell him first."

Against fires lighting up the yard, Tim saw that the girls were collecting dishes from the wounded. Apparently all had been fed.

"I'll go now," he said. "Be back in about a half an hour."

Tim rode Midnight past the parked wagons on to the road and headed north where White waited at the fork in the road. Though the forest on either side made the night seem inky black, above, the sky was studded with stars.

After having ridden for several hundred yards, Tim found his eyes adjusting to the dark. He pulled Midnight to a full stop. All was quiet ahead—too quiet. White, if he was alert at all, should have heard Tim's approach by this time. He gave a low whistle. No answer came from the vedette.

Tim dismounted. Alarmed now, he tethered Midnight to a bush, drew his pistol and headed warily for the division in the road just ahead. There was no sign of a horse, though White had taken his along. Of course, he may have tethered the mount off the road, Tim reasoned, but this close to the forked road, White should be clearly visible. But he was not there. Tim was alarmed at the situation.

"White!" he called in a low voice.

No answer.

Tim walked quickly to the vedette's post. He was nowhere in sight.

"White!" he called in a louder voice.

Still no answer.

Suddenly, in the dark still night, a low moan came from a thicket close behind. Tim whirled, dropped to his knees and covered the spot with his pistol, then he saw one boot sticking out of the brush. He jumped across the roadside ditch, swept aside the undergrowth, and knelt beside a shadowy prone figure. It was White!

Tim put an arm under the Ranger's shoulders and raised him to a sitting position.

"What happened?" he cried, but the Ranger was unconscious. Tim half-carried and half-dragged the man on to the road. When he put his hand on the wounded man's head, his fingers felt sticky.

For a moment Tim made no move, listening for possible suspicious sounds. Hearing none, he ran back to Midnight and brought her up. As quickly as he could, Tim draped the unconscious man over the saddle and swung up behind him. He sought desperately for some clue. It was unlikely that White had fallen off his horse, because a Ranger's horse was trained to stand, not run away. If Yankees had surprised the vedette, why did they leave him—and why had they not attacked the camp? He remembered the courier's warning. Bushwhackers! This was the way they would operate! He must warn Slaughter quickly.

Midnight, annoyed by the double burden, proved skittish.

"Behave yourself," Tim ordered, forcing his mare into a fast walk. Although feverishly anxious to warn the camp, he dared not gallop for fear of further hurting the wounded man.

Tim breathed a sigh of relief when he turned into the farmyard and saw the brightly burning fires, with Mrs.

McCarthy and her daughters still standing near the wounded men. They ought to be able to help them while he and Slaughter prepared for an attack. He urged Midnight on.

Just as Tim passed by the parked wagons, he saw a figure rouse himself to a sitting position.

"Run fer it, lad!" he heard Murphy yell.

"No, ye don't," growled a voice.

Two men jumped from behind a wagon, each with a pistol levelled at Tim's head.

"Git down or we'll shoot you outen thet saddle," one commanded. "And don't go fer thet pistol or you're a dead man," he added.

Tim's gaze swung back to the camp-fires, where several men who had been lying among the wounded, rose up from the ground.

"Git down, I said!" ordered one of his captors. He took a step forward, jerked the pistol from Tim's belt, then grabbed the boy's coat and hauled him off Midnight's back.

The men were dressed in clothing from both armies. One had on grey cavalry trousers of the Confederate Army and a faded red shirt, the other, a Union soldier's jacket and Rebel butternut trousers. They were unkempt, and, even in the dim light from the fire, Tim could see they were indescribably dirty.

"Bring 'im over here!" shouted a big man.

One of Tim's captors gave him a shove towards the fire, prodding him constantly with a pistol.

Tim searched vainly for Slaughter. He was nowhere in sight. As he approached the bull-like figure ahead, he could see the McCarthy women huddled together, their eyes wide with terror. Silently, Tim cursed himself for riding into camp like a blind fool, when he had every reason to expect a surprise attack.

"Well, lookee who we have here!" said a strangely familiar voice.

Tim stopped and stared at the corpulent ruffian. Bull Ruffing! Rage surged through Tim as he glowered at the man.

"Don't look so mad, sonny. Ya do like I tell ya and I might jist not shoot ya." He laughed heartily.

"Where's the sergeant?" Tim demanded.

Bull nodded to a limp form on the grass and said, "Now that's a warnin' fer ye, kid. He didn't do like I tole 'im, and look what he got."

"They slipped up on the camp, lad," called Murphy from his pallet. "The murderin' scum clubbed yer sergeant, brave man that he is, 'fore he got a chance to defend hisself."

"Wait'll the great Mosby hears we took a Ranger camp without firin' a shot," gloated Bull. "Too good fer the likes of us when we wanted to join up." He turned to Murphy. "And I ain't fergettin' ya tried to warn the kid." He walked over to the pallet and deliberately kicked the big Irishman in his wounded thigh.

Murphy groaned and doubled up in agony.

"You swine!" cried Tim and made a lunge for the bushwhacker.

One of Bull's men stuck out his foot, tripped the boy and levelled his pistol at him.

"Want I should drill 'im, Bull?" he asked.

Bull walked back and dragged Tim to his feet. He

held the boy at arm's length with one hand and slapped him brutally with the other.

Tim's knees buckled with the blow.

"Just a taste o' what yer gonna get," said Bull. He shoved the boy at one of the other bushwhackers, and ordered, "Tie 'im up and throw 'im in that smokehouse out back fer a while."

CHAPTER FOURTEEN

UNEXPECTED HELP

UNDER ORDINARY circumstances, the smokehouse would not have provided the security of a prison, but tied hand and foot, Tim was completely captive. Rage welled up in him as he remembered all the sorrow that Bull Ruffing had caused his family. His thoughts went back to Hank Slaughter's limp form on the ground, the unconscious White, so brutally dumped off Midnight's back. . . . And now his own plight! Obviously Bull meant to kill him and possibly all the wounded too. Bushwhackers seldom left witnesses.

As for Mrs. McCarthy and the two girls, Tim refused to let his thoughts dwell on their fate. He twisted his wrists violently, but the movement only sent a sharp pain through his arms. He moved his feet tentatively and decided those bonds were equally secure. Slowly he leaned back against the wall and tried to relax. He had to think—think hard. Anger and self-pity would only cloud his thoughts.

Bull Ruffing must have at least ten men in his gang, Tim figured. Against such odds, perhaps a half-dozen wounded Rangers, maybe more, could handle guns even though they were casualties. In addition, there were several Yankees who, if they could be trusted, would be of some assistance. Murphy he believed he could count on; the others, he didn't know.

Suddenly Tim realised that none of his planning would do any good unless he could get free. If only he had something sharp! Tim ran his hands over the rough planks behind him. A nail, almost any sharp metal, would help. Slowly he worked his way along each wall looking for an exposed nailhead. He covered all four walls and found none, then sat back exhausted, but still trying desperately to think of some means to get free.

At first he paid no attention to a slight rustling noise outside the smokehouse. Then a soft, feminine whisper in the darkness sent a wave of hope through him.

"Tim!"

He tried to locate the direction of the voice. "Where are you?" he whispered hoarsely.

"At the back of the smokehouse," came the urgent reply.

Tim rolled over to the back wall and stuck his face up against a crack in the timber.

"Who is it?" he called softly.

"It's me, Sarah," came the answer.

"Can you open the door?" Tim asked hopefully.

"I—I think so—I don't think it's locked."

"Hurry! Please try," pleaded Tim.

He heard a rustling sound, and soon the hinges squeaked as the door opened slowly.

"Where are you?" asked the girl.

"Against the back wall," Tim told her. "Do you have a knife?"

"Yes, Ma sent me to cut you loose." Once started, she talked rapidly. "Ma heard those men say they were going to kill you. When they sent us into the house, she told me to come and let you go. She said you could head up the hill at the back of the barn and hide in the woods."

"And let Ruffing kill the others?" Tim demanded angrily. "What does she think I am? Hurry," he added impatiently as the girl sawed away on the rope around his wrists.

"Here, let me have the knife," said Tim, when he felt the bonds loosen. He grabbed the blade and cut his ankles free. Jumping to his feet, he hurried to the door and looked out.

"I told Ma you wouldn't run," said Sarah softly.

"You're right," said Tim. "Where are the bushwhackers now?"

"They were going through the wagons last time I saw."

"What happened to the drivers?"

"When you came riding up, they were down on the ground with the wounded," answered the girl. "Those men made them lie down out of sight. Right now they're all together sitting in a circle by one of the wagons. There's a guard watching them."

"I've got to get some guns." He took the girl's hand and started out the door. "Let's get out of this place before someone comes back to check on me."

Swiftly the two ran across the yard to the darker shadows of the barn.

"Those awful men tied their horses behind the barn here when they sneaked up on the house," said the girl.

"That's it!" cried Tim. "Come on."

Hurriedly he dragged the girl around the old barn where the horses were tethered to a rail fence.

"Stay here," ordered Tim and ran quickly to the fence. He knew he had found one answer when he reached the first mount. A rifle rested snugly in the saddle boot. He found another on the second horse, but then it occurred to him that he needed pistols more than rifles. A quick search of the saddle-bags turned up half a dozen. Spares, he figured; bushwhackers were likely to carry any small weapons they could steal since those were easy to sell. Running back to the waiting girl, he showed her the armful of weapons.

"I've got to get these to some of the Rangers. You better slip back in the house now and keep out of the way. And—and thanks for helping me."

"How are you going to get the guns to your men?" asked the girl.

Tim thought for a minute.

"I'll have to go on the opposite side from the wagons and try to crawl among the wounded."

"Let me take them," said the girl.

"You! How on earth would you get guns to 'em?"

"Maybe I could walk out there with a bucket and a dipper and give the men a drink. I'll tell them Ma sent me."

"But how could you carry the pistols?" demanded Tim.

Sarah reached down, picked up the hem of her apron and doubled it under the waistband to form a pocket.

"I'll carry them in here."

"It might work," said Tim musingly.

"We can try it," answered the girl eagerly. "I'm not afraid."

Tim hesitated a minute. It seemed like a long chance

for a young girl to take with men as desperate as Bull Ruffing's gang. On the other hand, his own plan was hazardous and doubtful.

"All right," he said. "We'll try it. Give the pistols to the Rangers who seem well enough to sit up." He thought for a minute. "Give Sergeant Murphy one, too. I'll be at the corner of the house. If anything goes wrong, drop to the ground. I'll cover you with a rifle."

"How are you going to get Ruffing's gang away from the wagons so your men can see them?" Sarah asked.

"I don't know," answered Tim honestly. "We'll just have to wait until they go back towards the fire."

"After I pass out the guns, suppose I hide in the shadows and scream? That ought to bring them running."

Tim smiled in the darkness.

"We'd make you a general down South," he said with a chuckle. "You scream—but keep clear, hear me? And look—when you slip the men the guns, tell them to wait for my shot. That will be the signal for them to start shooting. Understand?"

"Yes," answered the girl. "Shall I go now? The bucket's there by the well."

"Good a time as any," said Tim. He stuffed the revolvers in the girl's apron. "Be careful now."

"I will," replied the girl and turned to go.

"Wait a minute." Tim caught her by the arm. "How do I know you won't give the pistols to Yankees?"

"You don't." She shook off his hand and hurried towards the well.

There was no way to stop the squeaking sound as Sarah raised the bucket from the well. Tim could only hope the bushwhackers were so busy inspecting the loot that they would not hear the noise. He waited until Sarah had the bucket and had started around one side of the house; then he ran silently around the other.

The fires blazed merrily, indeed; as far as Tim was concerned, they gave off far too much light. So much, in fact, that if Sarah wasn't extremely careful, one of Ruffing's gang was sure to notice the guns.

"Hey you! Where do you think you're going?" A burly member of the gang challenged the girl when she appeared among the wounded. Tim, hiding behind the porch, drew a bead on the challenger.

"Ma says I'm to give these men a drink," answered the girl with feigned sweetness.

"Hey, Bull!" the man called. "You want I should let this gal give 'em a drink?"

"Why sure, Bart. We gotta take care of 'em. They're sick men!" Bull laughed uproariously, the other bushwhackers joining in. Obviously they were in great spirits over the immense value of the wagon-train loot.

Tim saw Sarah pick her way among the sprawling men. She stopped by one, dropped to her knees and ladled a dipper of water from the bucket. As she held it to the Ranger's lips, Tim watched her lean close to his head. The man drank, then sank back on his blanket, as the girl passed on to the next trooper.

At last she placed the bucket on the ground and walked into the shadows beyond the fire.

Tim glanced again at the wagon park, and saw Ruffing and his gang gleefully gloating over a box they had just broken open. Obviously they had found something of great value in it.

Suddenly, a shrill scream rang out through the camp. Tim's spine tingled. Sarah sure was a good actress. He gripped his rifle and covered the group of bushwhackers.

"What's the matter with that fool girl?" yelled Ruffing. He stalked towards the camp, turned his course towards the screaming voice, his men following. The one called Bart ran towards the girl. Tim followed him with his rifle muzzle until he had almost reached her.

Wham! The rifle jumped in Tim's hands and Bart dropped.

Tim's shot started a wild fusillade of shots. Rangers sat up and emptied their pistols at the gang around Ruffing. A few bushwhackers, startled as they were, snatched for their guns, but the deadly Ranger fire prevented the return of a single shot.

Tim saw Ruffing break for the shadows. He snapped a quick shot at the fleeing bully and saw him stumble. He dashed from his hiding place and raced to the fallen man.

"Don't shoot! Don't shoot!" shrieked Bull. "I'm dyin' already."

Covering him, Tim leaned down and in the half-light looked at the man's wound. The bullet had passed through the flesh of the deserter's leg. A minor wound only, Tim saw with satisfaction; Ruffing would live to be hanged.

"You'll live, Bull Ruffing," promised Tim grimly. "At least until I can turn you over to Major Mosby." He picked up the bushwhacker's pistol that had fallen a few feet away.

"On your feet!"

"I can't! I'm wounded, I tell you," groaned Bull,

Tim centred the bore of his rifle on the man's forehead. "Try," he suggested softly. "If you can't walk, I'll put you out of your misery right here."

"Don't shoot," screamed Bull. "I'll walk." He struggled to his feet, groaning with the pain.

"Back to the camp-fire."

Bull limped to the centre of the camp and dropped exhaustedly to the ground.

Murphy sat on his blanket, a revolver in his hand. "Neatly planned, lad. There's never a one to bother ye now," he said. Then, "Niver ye mind this one," he nodded towards Bull. "I'll see that he makes no move."

Tim glanced around the camp. "Where's Hank?" he asked.

"Over here, Tim," the sergeant shouted. "Come git these dang ropes off'n me."

Tim ran to the sergeant and quickly untied his bonds.

"Hank, I thought sure they'd killed you," cried the boy happily.

"That Ruffing bent a pistol barrel over my head," Hank said, touching his head gingerly, "and I'm gettin' fed up with Yankee's tryin' to crack my skull!"

He shook off the loosed bonds and walked ominously towards the leader of the gang. "Let me see how hard Ruffing's head is!"

"Don't hit me!" yelled Ruffing. "I'm a wounded man!"

Hank stared coldly at the cringing bushwhacker. "It's only because I want to watch you hang that I don't bend a rifle across your head," he said angrily. He turned to Tim. "Let's get organised again, Tim."

"White's hurt," Tim said. He nodded towards a limp figure near the wagons. "He's still over there where they dumped him."

Hank hurried over to the vedette. He felt the man's pulse, then stood up slowly. Sadly he walked back to Tim. "He's dead," he said quietly.

Hank turned hate-filled eyes on Ruffing. "One more count against you, bushwhacker," he said coldly.

"We gonna stay here, Hank?" asked another Ranger from the ground. "Seems like we'd be better off movin'."

"That's what I aim to do," answered the sergeant. "Where are the drivers?" His eyes searched the camp.

"I'll see what I can round up," offered Tim.

He headed for the wagon park, then suddenly stopped. Where had Sarah gone? Tim looked around the camp and finally saw her standing in the shadows by a tree. He hurried over to her.

"I want to thank you, Miss Sarah," he said. "I think it was——"

"I didn't do it for you, Rebel," the girl snapped. "I wanted to save our own wounded." She brushed by the young Ranger and hurried to her mother, who had just come out of the house.

Tim stared after the girl in astonishment. Of all the changeable females, he thought, as anger grew in him. Not half an hour ago she had saved him from sure death. Now she wouldn't even listen to his thanks. What was the matter with girls? Perplexed, he hurried towards the wagon park.

CHAPTER FIFTEEN

THE 43RD TO THE RESCUE

"I CAN ONLY find four, Hank," said Tim, nodding towards the drivers he had rounded up.

"Where are the others?" demanded the sergeant.

"They headed for the woods," answered one of the drivers.

"How come you didn't light out, too?"

The civilian glanced at the bodies of Ruffing's cutthroats. "To tell you the truth," he said, "I don't know which is worse, workin' fer a Rebel or maybe runnin' into more like that gang."

Hank thought for a minute, then spoke to Tim. "Let's get hitched up. Those drivers'll have Yankees on us first chance they get." He threw a contemptuous look at the dead bushwhackers. "Guess we'll have to tote 'em along."

" 'Deed you will!" said Mrs. McCarthy as she came striding up to them. "You won't leave or bury 'em on my farm," she said.

Hank pacified the woman. "We'll take 'em along, ma'am. How about you? You and the girls want to go along with us 'til we find some neighbours?"

"We stay here."

Hank shot a glance at the two young girls who had come up behind their mother.

"Don't you think——"

"We stay here," the woman insisted flatly. "We ain't afraid. This is our home and we ain't leavin'."

"Very well, ma'am," said Hank. "We'd best be gettin' along." He turned to the drivers and ordered, "Get hitched up. . . . And, Tim, see if any of our boys are strong enough to drive teams."

"If I can hold a pistol, I reckon I can hold the reins of a team," answered one Ranger when Tim canvassed the wounded men. "Just prop me up behind the seat and I'll keep 'em movin'."

With only four men it took considerable time to get the teams in place. Hank chafed at the delay. Half the night was gone, and he wanted to get across the mountain pass pointed out by the courier before daylight. He ranged up and down the park, driving the sweating men to greater speed. Suddenly he stiffened, eyes searching the darkness beyond.

"Tim," he called in a low, urgent voice.

Surprised at the sudden change in his sergeant's voice, Tim left the team he had been helping.

"What's the matter?" he asked.

"I dunno," Hank said slowly. "All at once I gotta feeling someone's watchin'."

Tim stared into the darkness uncertainly.

"Come with me." Hank moved away from the wagons and the noise of the teams and drivers.

The two Rangers had almost reached the road when Hank stopped again in the darkness.

"Hear anything?"

Tim listened intently. "Not a thing," he answered.

"Me neither," whispered the sergeant. "Coupla

tree frogs yellin' their heads off a while back. Now I don't hear a sound."

Suddenly a voice boomed out of the darkness along the road.

"Sergeant Slaughter!"

Both Rangers spun, drew their pistols and dropped flat on the ground.

"Sergeant Slaughter!" the voice rang out again.

"Holy mackerel!" yelled Tim, jumping to his feet. "That's the Major!"

"Yes, sir, Major, here we are!"

Now came the sound of many horses on the road below, and in less than a minute the Partisan chief's big grey trotted into the yard. Jubilant voices were raised as their chief rode up to the camp-fire.

Mosby swung off his mount and stared at the bodies of Ruffing's gang. He turned to Slaughter.

"We found your vedette on the road south of here. What happened?" he demanded.

The twenty Rangers who had ridden in with Mosby remained deathly silent as Hank told about the wagon train's capture by Ruffing and his gang, and the subsequent fight for freedom. When Hank pointed out Ruffing to the Major, all the Rangers turned cold eyes on the bushwhacker.

"We'll take care of him," Mosby said coldly. Then, turning to his men, "help our wounded into the wagons. . . . We'll leave the Yankees here."

Mosby spied Mrs. McCarthy, flanked by her two daughters, standing near the porch of their home. He walked briskly up to the woman and removed his hat with a flourish.

"Ma'am," he said, "I am Major Mosby of the 43rd Ranger Battalion. Please accept my gratitude for your assistance to my men. You are most kind to extend aid to the enemy."

The woman pushed at a stray curl in embarrassment, as the Major bowed politely.

" 'Tain't fitten to neglect the sick," she said piously.

Tim stared in amazement at the change in the iron-willed Mrs. McCarthy. The Major sure had a way with the ladies, he reflected. He was now turning his attention to the daughters.

"You young ladies have also earned my deepest gratitude."

This is a Rebel that Sarah doesn't seem to hate, Tim thought, as the girls curtsied, obviously enthralled by the Major's courtly bearing and resplendent uniform. He wondered if *he* were an officer, would Sarah look as admiringly at him.

Further speculation on the subject was brought to an abrupt halt by Slaughter, who put Tim to work helping the wounded Rangers into the wagons.

"Good thing the 43rd was headed south again when the courier got over into the next valley," Hank said. "Did you hear the Major say General Stuart was there, too?"

"Uh huh," said Tim absently.

Hank looked at him sharply. "What's got into you, boy?"

"Nothing," mumbled Tim.

The sergeant decided to let it go at that.

It took the Rangers very little time to get the wagon

train ready. Mosby waited until all was in readiness, then walked slowly over to the Yankee wounded by the camp-fire.

"You men will not have to remain here long," he said. "Mrs. McCarthy has offered to take care of you until help arrives. I will send word to the nearest Federal command that you are here. We have left medical supplies for you."

"Thank ye, Major," replied Murphy, as he raised himself to a sitting position on his blanket.

Mosby then levelled his ice-blue eyes on Ruffing.

"Put this man under guard in one of the wagons," he said, without turning, to two Rangers at his rear.

"Beggin' yer pardon, Major," said Murphy, "but I'll be takin' this man to justice."

Mosby glanced at the Yankee sergeant. "I'm sorry, Sergeant, but we'll settle with him."

Suddenly there was a gun in Murphy's hand. It was pointed directly at the Major.

" 'Tis me duty, sor, to take this man in," he said flatly.

Mosby gazed steadily at the gun and then at the Irishman's face. The camp had become deadly quiet. Silently the Rangers spread out, eyes riveted on Murphy's weapon.

Mosby stared coldly at the Yankee sergeant.

"Do you realise there are at least twenty guns here to your one," he demanded. "If I raise my hand, you'll be a dead man."

"Both of us will, sor," Murphy amended quietly.

Mosby stared at the man in exasperation, but showed absolutely no fear of the gun in Murphy's hand.

"Either you are a fool or a very brave man. Why do you want this ruffian?"

" 'Tis me duty, sor," said the Yankee sergeant. "He's wanted for desertion in time of war, and theft—perhaps murder."

Mosby thought for a minute, then called over his shoulder, "Morgan, step up here."

Tim moved up beside him and, staring down at the gun in Murphy's hand, did not doubt that the sergeant would use it.

"You captured Ruffing. Do you think the Irishman will turn him over to the authorities for proper punishment?"

Tim looked at Murphy. Grim determination was written on the sergeant's face.

"Yes, Major," he replied. "I know he will."

"All right, men. Roll 'em out." Mosby turned on his heel, walked to his big grey, and mounted.

Tim, with a backward smile at Murphy, walked to Midnight and swung into his saddle.

"Morgan!"

Tim jumped at the sharp voice.

"Have you thanked the young lady for her help?"

Tim's face reddened. "Well, sir, I——"

"I suggest you mind your manners," Mosby said. He raised his hand and cried, "Let 'em roll," then galloped to the head of the wagon train.

Tim turned Midnight and walked her to the farmhouse where Sarah stood watching the wagon train from the bottom step. He rode slowly up, dismounted, and took off his hat.

"Miss Sarah, whether you want thanks or not, I

reckon I have to tell you anyway that I am mighty grateful for your help." He twisted his hat in his hands nervously. "I think you were mighty brave," he went on with a rush, "and I'm sorry we're on different sides and there's a war going on."

Sarah smiled and held out her hand.

"I'm glad I could help you, Tim," she said looking directly in his eyes. "The war won't last forever."

"No."

Tim wanted to say more. He wanted to say something about the strange feeling in his chest, but he couldn't find the words. He turned, swung into the saddle, and kneed Midnight into a gallop. He looked back once at the slim, graceful figure. She was right; the war couldn't last forever, and maybe he'd get back to Maryland again. . . .